To Aaron,
for continuing to gently push me.

CHAPTER 1

My mind was all over the place. My left shoulder was staying put.

Staying put … put … put … okay, it just moved a half inch closer to what they call the agony of defeat.

But back to my roving mind. I was thinking of girl-of-my-dreams Laurie Middlebrook … the broken light in the wrestling room's rafters that never seems to get fixed and that I could see through my squinted eyes … and an unknown odor wafting off my opponent.

Oops! My left shoulder just gave way another half inch.

Yeah, I was on my back and struggling like an upside-down turtle in the middle of the road while trying not to get pinned at wrestling practice. And yet my concentration was being broken by that strange smell that one might associate with a please-pick-me participant on "The Bachelor." Not that I ever watched that silly show — at least not a whole episode.

So what was that all about? Wrestling rooms are supposed to smell like Icy Hot, unwashed uniforms and a big vat of adolescent hormones and sweat. Not the girls' side of the cafeteria at a junior high dance.

Another half inch.

I couldn't even muster up enough thoughts of the lovely Laurie to inspire me to break the smell-from-heck spell. (I wish I could rhyme that better but I'm not into cussing yet.) The only thing keeping me from getting pinned was my left shoulder staying off the mat and …

Thud!

That was Coach Mathews slamming his hand down on the gym floor to signal a pin. My shoulder had finally given way just as my stomach felt like evicting my lunch — if you can call a few baby carrots and a small bag of Doritos a lunch.

"Hey, you made a nice escape move before I took you down, Spank," my opponent said as she held out her hand to help me up.

You heard me right. She. I'll get to that soon enough.

I do know that I didn't need any compliments from her.

"Yeah, well, I might have done a little better if you hadn't tried to poison the air around here," I told her. "I'm surprised some of the other guys haven't fallen over in some kind of stupor. What is that anyway?"

"It sure isn't perspiration since it only took me about 45 seconds to pin you," she answered, showing her true self. "It's called perfume. Maybe you should let me give you a couple of squirts if you think it gives me an advantage."

A lot of our teammates must have heard her smart comments as we walked off the mat. Actually, she skipped. They started laughing and giving me a hard time. I even thought I saw Coach Mathews trying to hide a smile. A little levity at practice can be a good thing, but too much of it seems to come at somebody's expense — too many times mine — thanks to the girl we call Wheat.

Weighing 113 pounds on most days, I was again starting to wonder if I ought to find another way to utilize my lack of size, and strength, other than the sport of wrestling.

I should probably introduce myself. The whole shebang is William Raymond Rogers. But it's Billy Ray for short. My grandpas are William and Raymond and so that's how that came about. But just about everybody besides teachers and other serious-minded adults calls me Spanky. Or Spank. Or the Spanker.

I'm 15 years old and a sophomore at Clay High School in South Bend, Indiana —home of the Fighting Irish of Notre Dame that you may have heard of. I live with my mom, who has been a kindergarten teacher, and my step-father, a police officer. They got married when I was 11, four years after my real dad died. I got a sister in the deal, too. She is just 12 days younger than I am and usually right about the same weight as me.

I know her weight because we get on the scales before every practice ... when we get up in the morning ... when we go to bed at night ... and after every meal. Sometimes, I even weigh myself after I go No. 1 just so I can feel good about losing a few more ounces. Keeping an eagle eye on your weight is a pretty big deal to a wrestler.

And yeah, my step-sister (although we really don't look at each other as steps) is the girl who pinned me yet again at practice. Might as well tell you that she just about always beats me when we square off. Too bad we are in the same weight class. She is a pint-sized version of Wonder Woman — or one of those Ninja Warriors. Or maybe even that good-looking girl elf from "The Hobbit."

In fact, she probably is the best girl wrestler in the whole state of Indiana. And against the boys in the 113-pound class, she is 15-2 so far this season.

Her real name is Tanda Lea Evans but everybody pretty much calls her Wheat. No, not because she is skinny like a stalk of wheat or anything like that. Her dad nicknamed her that because her sometimes crazy hair reminded him of the girl in an old TV show called "The Little Rascals." That girl was called Buckwheat but nobody wants a name that long and it apparently has some racial overtones these days. Don't want anything like that. So she quickly became just Wheat.

I never heard about The Little Rascals until my step-dad and Tanda moved in with Mom and me. I guess because my step-dad already had a Buckwheat, he decided he might as well raise a Spanky, too. Spanky was also a Little Rascal — kind of a chubby, goofy-looking kid with a beanie who always wanted to be in charge. Nothing like me. But anyway, that's how I got my nickname.

I wish I had a better story than that to tell you about our nicknames. But I don't. I don't mind mine. I just don't think I want to be a Spanky when I'm older — like maybe when I turn 18.

We are what some people call a blended family. My mom, whose name is Louise — or Loosey Goosey as my step-dad sometimes calls her — is white like me. In fact, we are almost too white. Both of us burn easily in the sun and need to wear hats and lots of sunscreen when we're outside for any amount of time in the summer. I don't tell her this, but Mom looks really good in her Chicago Cub cap with a pony tail sticking out the back. I don't know why, but I love girls in baseball caps.

My step-dad, whose name is Ric Evans, is a tall Black guy who looks a little like that movie star Dwayne Johnson who used to be The Rock. And I would give Ric a fighting chance against The Rock. He's one strong dude.

Tanda, or Wheat, is sort of in between in color. Her real mom is mostly Hawaiian but we don't see her. Wheat and Ric – I'm starting to call him Dad here and there – aren't even sure where she is anymore. That's okay. I like the family just the way it is.

Yeah, I do like Wheat. I prefer my buddies don't know that I like her all that much, though. But she is probably my best friend, even if she can beat me up on the wrestling mat just about any time she wants.

We're in the same grade at school and also in the same algebra class. For now, we even share a bedroom at home, but we don't broadcast that. We have a 20-month-old brother named Lake — oops, should have mentioned him before — and he has what used to be Wheat's room, now called a nursery. She moved into my room for what was supposed to be a few months after Lake was born.

I didn't like it at first. But she didn't mind taking the top bunk and we have gotten used to each other as roommates. My parents gave me the choice about a year ago: I could room with Lake or keep sharing with Wheat. I think they were surprised when I picked Wheat.

I think they were even a little sorry that they even made that one of the choices. If Lake was a little older, I might have picked him but he's still in diapers and ... you know. I like little kids but not enough to get involved with that kind of stuff. He also starts talking to himself about 5 in the morning and I don't need that.

And Wheat didn't mess with my decor (that's the word, right?) Like my collection of frogs — plastic, ceramic and a couple of real ones called Notre and Dame that I keep in aquariums — and my big posters of former Chicago Cub players Anthony Rizzo and Kris Bryant. I'm still sick about them getting traded and don't have the heart to take them down.

"They're cute," Wheat said of both the frogs and the ex-Cubs.

So we were good.

I know a lot of the guys think Wheat is pretty and I suppose she is in a weird sort of way. But she might as well be a guy as far as I'm concerned. Neither one of us is into that girl-boy stuff. That's what I keep telling myself anyway — until that girl named Laurie Middlebrook pops into my mind.

That doesn't mean we go into the bathroom together or talk about stuff like puberty (that was uncomfortable enough in ninth grade health class) but I don't care if she sees me in my underwear or anything. Hey, she's my sister and we've been together for four years now.

And we spend more time wrapped up in practice than some of those fake love scenes in the movies. I know that sounds weird. Actually, it sounds kind of yucky now that I put it in words. But, hey, that's wrestling. It's a sport that takes some people a little time to get used to — my mom included.

A lot of guys don't like wrestling Wheat. I think more because she can beat them rather than that they don't want to wrestle a girl. Most of our teammates have gotten over it, though. Even if she is a girl and just a sophomore, she is one of the leaders on the team.

We're moving pretty soon. At least that's our parents' plans. They're even thinking about putting in an offer on a new house that's sort of out in the country and I'm okay with that. Right now, we live next door to a funeral home — a neat old white house with a couple of big pillars by the front door and black shutters on all its windows. That's part of the reason they've wanted to move, thinking it might seem a little creepy raising a family next to a funeral home. But I haven't minded.

The funeral directors, two brothers named Todd and Michael Dixon, pay me to shovel the snow off their paths, mow their yard and occasionally wash their big cars when no mourners are around for me to accidentally squirt. I even know the combination to their garage so I can get into the place for the snow shovels and lawnmower.

They have a basketball goal out back in the far end of their parking lot and they let us use it when they aren't having a visitation or a funeral. Both of the Dixons played high school basketball and sometimes they will play one-on-one while in their loosened ties and dress shoes. They laugh and cuss at each other like they're still young guys.

They're funny, too, which most people would never guess about funeral directors. Todd — although I call them both Mr. Dixon — is always singing old cowboy songs like "keep those dogies rollin', Rawhide," and goofy stuff like that. And Michael will sometimes walk around on his hands after basketball. You can't believe all the loose change I've found that's fallen out of his pockets and into the grass. So I haven't minded at all living next to them.

But my parents also want a bigger house — and the one they're seriously considering is an old redone farmhouse. We've all seen it and, yeah, I like it. But I think maybe the main reason my parents want to move is so Wheat and I can have our own rooms. I guess I wouldn't mind my own room again. But I would miss my talks with Wheat at night. We can get pretty serious. Of course, we can be silly, too.

I like to stick my feet up into her mattress springs and lift her up in the air. I don't want to do that too much, though. She has this knack of swinging down the side of the top bunk like one of those Indians on a horse in the old Westerns. (We see a lot of old movies because Ric is a Hollywood aficionado.) Then she'll swat me. And like I said, she can whip me in just about anything physical.

That took a little getting used to. We're both kind of scrawny – me even more so, I guess, since I'm the guy. Her real mom — DeeDee is her name — was a fairly famous surfer and Ric played football in college at Northern Illinois before becoming an Army Ranger and then a cop. Being athletic is in Wheat's genes.

I'm still trying to find out what sports I might be good at. I was so bad in Little League that I got the Most Improved Award two years in a row and I still was lousy. I know I'm hopeless at basketball. And wrestling? I guess I'm sort of okay.

If it wasn't for Wheat, I would probably be wrestling varsity at 113 pounds. But that's because the only other kid in our weight class, Tommy Reston, is out for the team because his dad made him. I don't have to do much more than say boo to take him down. He is good for my ego. Teammates call him Tommy the Torso. He is built like a pipe cleaner but he seems to like his nickname. I think it makes him feel like he belongs. I suppose it does.

I mainly like to wrestle so I can get to be around Wheat and watch how good she continues to get. She just has the knack and works really, really hard at it. I should point out that Ric's brother, Uncle Mason, has two sons — our cousins — who were All-State wrestlers over in Illinois. Ric and Wheat lived with them for a year after Wheat's mom took off with her surfboard and some guy she called The Bubber.

Ric says that Wheat used to follow her cousins around like a puppy. They eventually quit ignoring her and taught her all about wrestling and weight training and being really aggressive when somebody is trying to turn you upside down.

I don't think they taught her about wearing perfume while she wrestled, though.

So when we got in our beds, I finally asked her about it.

"Seriously, what was that stuff you were wearing at practice today?"

"It's called Midnight Breeze," she answered. "Did you like it?"

"Probably as much as I like mat burns. And I don't think you've been up past midnight since I've known you. So is this some sort of a statement by you that a girl who wrestles can still be feminine?"

"Nope. I call it a competitive advantage."

"Explain."

"Okay, when I was just about to pin you today, what were you thinking about?" Wheat went on.

- 8 -

I wasn't going to mention Laurie Middlebrook, that was for sure. "Well, besides trying desperately to keep my back from being flat off the mat, I guess I was wondering why the heck you would be wearing perfume at wrestling practice."

"Exactly. Your mind wasn't entirely on how you were going to get out of my hold. Wrestling didn't have your full concentration. Not that I need any kind of advantage to beat you — ha, ha. But it might help me against a really competitive opponent."

Unlike Tommy the Torso, Wheat is not always great for my ego, but she has made me a better wrestler. Heck, I wouldn't even be wresting at all if it wasn't for her. When she was competing against the boys at Junior Olympic events when our family was first formed, I got dragged along. I eventually figured out it was better being on the mat than up doing nothing in the stands.

I decided not to respond to her last comment about a "competitive opponent," but I did use my feet to push her and her mattress about a foot from the ceiling. She yelled and I lowered her down before she could come after me.

"Midnight Breeze," I grumbled. "Not exactly you."

"Well, I may stay awake past midnight just to show you," she said. "But you sleep tight, Spanker."

"Back at you, Stinker."

I should probably tell you that we like making up even more nicknames for ourselves — most of them pretty lame.

CHAPTER 2

We got up at 5:45 the next morning and ran four miles before breakfast. We do that on most mornings. Why? Wheat says that's what wrestlers do. It does help us keep our weight down for one thing and it improves our endurance. It can interrupt some pretty good dreams, though.

A lot of the other guys on the team will run over in the gym at lunchtime if they need to shed some pounds to get down to their weight requirement before a meet. I'm glad to get it over with in the morning. I don't want to smell in English class right after lunch because I sit beside Laurie Middlebrook, our mayor's daughter and one of the cutest girls in our sophomore class. Have I mentioned her before?

If Ric hasn't worked his part-time security job the previous night, he usually will join us on my bicycle if the snow isn't too bad on the streets. He's way too big for it but it's too early in the morning to find any humor in how he looks. Even so, his knees sometimes hit the handlebars when he pedals. It sounds like it should hurt a lot but he never says anything, at least about that.

He does keep the conversation going. Wheat and I don't say too much and we act like we aren't interested in what he's saying as we jog through the darkness. But Ric does know a lot of stuff. I guess that's one good thing about being old.

I do hate it when he starts singing some of his Airborne Ranger songs, though. What a racket. Wheat yells at him to stop but I save my breath. I do know that nobody is going to mess with us when Ric is around. He is 6-foot-3 and 225 pounds of muscle. And I think he usually carries his pistol in his fanny pack — or whatever macho guys call those things that wrap around your waist.

For breakfast, and most other meals, we put what we eat on a little scale that Mom got for us. We don't count calories. We count ounces. Occasionally, I have to lose a pound or two before my junior varsity meets and Wheat wants to make sure she is staying a little under 112 pounds.

Coach Mathews wondered if I wanted to try to lose enough weight to wrestle varsity at 106 pounds, our lowest class. No, I didn't, I told him. I'm usually pretty accommodating, but not for that. I already look skinny enough.

Billy Thurston is our only 106-pounder and I can tie him up like a pretzel. He and Tommy the Torso are made for each other as wrestling partners during practice. But if I weighed what Billy weighs, I don't think I would be much better than he is. We usually call him Thirsty Thurston because he can drink more water than a camel after practice.

He only weighs 97 pounds so he doesn't have to worry about losing weight. Sometimes, I think he drinks too much water, just because he wants to live up to his nickname. He always seems to have to run off to the bathroom halfway through practice. Coach Mathews just shakes his head and sometimes calls Thirsty "a No. 1 pain." Get it?

Actually, there had been some talk before the season about Wheat wrestling at 106 pounds. Coach Mathews thought she would have a good shot at a state title. But Ric stepped in and said he didn't want her doing that. He pointed out that Wheat had very little body fat as it was and he thought that kind of weight loss – even if was just for the days of the meets – would not be healthy. Coach Mathews understood.

Wheat's 5-foot-4 frame is pretty much all muscle. And as Ric once said, "There isn't too much 'sugar and spice and everything nice' in that girl." That's from a really old nursery rhyme, I think.

So both Wheat and I usually don't have to cut a lot of weight like some of the guys. We have a meet tonight against Adams High School, a crosstown rival. Wheat may have a tough match. She beat her guy at the holiday tourney, just 4-2, and you could tell he didn't like losing to her. He kicked over a few folding chairs on his way to the locker room after the match.

I should have an easier time with my opponent in the junior varsity. I pinned him in the second period at the county JV invitational. Like I said, I'm not terrible.

I've been more nervous about a book report I have to give in my advanced English class. There are 19 girls and only four guys in that class and that sort of gives me the woolies. You would think that with me doing so much with Wheat that I would be okay with a bunch of girls around me. It obviously doesn't work that way, though.

I usually get a frog in my throat — the only kind of frog I don't like to collect — and it's hard to clear it when I have to talk in English class. Besides, Laurie Middlebrook is in there and sits right beside me. Blonde, blue-eyed and I'm guessing in the 120-pound category if she was a wrestler.

"You'll do fine," Wheat said as we walked to the corner so Big Jim Guffie could pick us up.

Big Jim is a senior and the heavyweight on the wrestling team. We pay him a couple dollars a week to drive us to school. He is also an offensive lineman on the football team and weighs a lot more than Wheat and I put together.

He's a good guy but he's not real big in the personal hygiene department. Who knows, maybe he has big sweat glands, too. Coach Mathews actually made him take his uniform home to wash a couple of weeks ago. That was kind of embarrassing. Maybe Wheat could introduce him to some Midnight Breeze — ha, ha.

Fortunately, we ride in the backseat because his sister Sally sits shotgun, usually with the window cracked. She's a junior and thinks she's hot stuff — which she pretty much is. She is a varsity cheerleader and usually ignores Wheat and me. But for some reason, she was in a talking mood.

"One of my friends asked me if you're the little girl who wrestles and who they call Wheat," Sally said. "I knew you wrestled but I didn't know they called you Wheat."

"Some of my friends do," Wheat answered.

"Boys, right?" Sally continued with a smile on her face. "With your wrestling, you probably don't get a chance to do a lot of stuff with girls."

"None like you," Wheat answered and smiled back.

"Yeah, I could see that," Sally said.

I was getting a little nervous. One thing that Wheat hates is somebody who thinks she's better than others.

But before anything else was said, Big Jim leaned over and punched his sister in the shoulder. I guess he had to wait until he had turned the corner and could get a hand free. He may be a bit of a slob but he is a careful driver.

Sally let out a yell.

"That was totally unnecessary, you big jerk," she squawked. "I'm putting your toothbrush in the toilet for a few laps, if you even have one. Then I'm telling dad."

"Go ahead, Sis," he said. "Just lay off Wheat. I might not be able to hold her back if she gets really mad at you. Maybe I wouldn't even try that hard. And I bet more guys would rather take her to the winter formal than you."

Those appeared to be fighting words to Sally.

"Is that right, Mr. Lord of the Dance? I've already turned down a couple of guys. And I've heard that I have a couple others waiting to ask me. But I'm sure that little girl in the back seat could get somebody to take her. She's pretty cute."

"Not really into dances," Wheat said while I watched her sort of squeeze her fists.

"How about we ask Little Mister Quiet back there," Sally said, while she turned around and looked me over. "You got an opinion on all this?"

Well, of course, I did. I thought Sally was maybe the prettiest girl at school but meaner than a rattle snake. I figured that about an hour of her big brother sticking her head in his armpit would do her some good.

She's about 5-foot-7, has dark brown hair that twirls at the end and the neatest green eyes I've ever seen. Don't most snakes have green eyes? I guess she would be a 132-pounder if she had a weight class and she is equipped with a lot more curves than straight lines. Too many for me to try to take in, I'll be honest. I would give her looks the strongest of 9's on my 10-point scale but her personality would drop her to an overall rating of 4.

But I decided to be diplomatic.

"I think you're pretty enough to be the winter formal's queen," I said.

Big Jim started laughing. Wheat gave me a quick elbow in the gut. And Sally was speechless for a moment — but just a moment.

"Well, aren't you the little charmer?" she said. "I might keep an eye on you in case you ever develop out of your Tiny Tim stage. So if you're the magic mirror on the wall, who's the fairest of them all?"

"Laurie Middlebrook is Snow White as far as my brother is concerned," Wheat answered before I could say anything. "You're probably just one of the many also-rans on the runway in his dreams."

"That's not true," I protested. "I don't like girls. Any girls. Especially not this idiot sitting beside me."

By that time, Big Jim had pulled into the school parking lot. I got out of the car fuming. But before I could slam the door, Sally grabbed me by my coat collar and pulled me up against her. Then she planted a kiss right on my lips in front of the whole school – or at least 20 or so passers-by.

"You know, I could make you forget Laurie Middlebrook if I wanted to, Little Man," she said before finally letting go of my coat.

I felt like the frog in the fairytale and I guess I did change in looks — turning all red and sweaty. I figured if she gave me any more kisses like that, I might forget my own name. I wouldn't care if one of her smackeroos turned me into Prince Charming — or a frog. But then she let out what I can only call a harpy laugh, waved at a couple of her friends and left me in her dust.

"Geez, Spank," Big Jim said. "That's what you get for saying something nice to my sister. She is terminally evil and a lot rougher than you might think. Back when we were kids, she could almost battle me to a draw with her dirty tactics. And now, she might have you on her list. Good luck with that. She's not normal."

"I think I might be jogging to school from now on," I said and then went running after a giggling Wheat.

CHAPTER 3

I should tell you right now that I have never been much of a ladies' man. Maybe I will be someday but not at the moment. Hey, I'm only 15. I like girls probably a little more than I want to admit but when you are smaller than a lot of the ones your own age, you kinda have to resort to admire them from afar.

I did kiss a few girls at an eighth grade party down in Sandy Wendle's basement when we played spin the bottle. Although I think I kind of liked those smooches, I was a little unsettled by the whole experience, maybe because other people were watching and egging everyone on. But that smacker that Sally Guffie put on me ... well, I felt it all the way down to my toes and back up to my ears. That was a totally new experience for me.

I never did catch Wheat as I chased her into school – yeah, she's faster than me, too – but all I really wanted to do was ask her how she knew I had a bit of a crush on Laurie Middlebrook. It's not like I've carved her name into our bedroom wall or anything. Maybe I've doodled down her name once or twice, I don't know.

I don't think I talk in my sleep, which wouldn't be good, because about half my dreams are about Laurie. Most of the other half are about me suddenly realizing that I'm sitting in English class in just my underwear. But those are sort of about Laurie, too, since I sit beside her.

I don't really like Sally Guffie any more than I did – maybe I even dislike her more now – but I'm thinking I might start having a few dreams about those ruby red lips of hers, too. Okay, maybe they weren't ruby red, but I like how that sounds.

I thought about that kiss all morning, hardly giving a thought to our meet that night. I even got caught daydreaming in algebra class and Mr. Rammel, one of my favorite teachers, got on me a little. Oh, well, we Romeos have a lot on our plate — ha, ha.

Speaking of plates, there wasn't much on mine at lunch since I was a pound heavy in the morning. I ate a few celery sticks I had packed and some kind of nutty bar I got out of a machine in the cafeteria.

When I walked into English class, I did my usual. I nodded to my buddy, Bobby Taylor, said a "Hello, Mrs. Murphy" to our teacher like the good boy that I am and then tried to look over at Laurie Middlebrook in a casual sort of way, even though we're talking about the highlight of my day when I sit down beside her.

She is always pretty nice to me. We sometimes even say a few words with my heart pounding about two hundred times a minute. I call that my Hummingbird Heart. And then the business of English takes over. Laurie is a serious straight-A type student. I'm pretty close, just not in her league. In pretty much anything.

But I almost stopped in my tracks when I looked at her this time. She was staring right at me like she had been waiting for me to walk into the class. Then she gave me this shy smile and quickly looked away. Uh-oh. Somebody must have announced my little secret to her. I'm sure it wasn't Wheat, which meant it probably was Sally Guffie or one of her friends.

I started sweating all over, which was good in some ways because of the weight I needed to lose. I never looked Laurie's ways the whole class and when I gave my five-minute book report, I started out sounding like a soprano.

Bobby and some of the other kids even laughed a little before Mrs. Murphy gave them The Stare. She is famous for that. Then they got kind of bored. It's pretty hard to jazz up <u>The Grapes of Wrath</u>.

That 55-minute period seemed to drag on for days before the bell finally rang. I was planning on getting out of there lickety-split but I felt a pull on one of my back belt loops as I stood up. I looked around and to my surprise ... my horror ... and my ecstasy, Laurie was holding it.

"Walk me down the hallway, would you Spank?" she asked.

I didn't faint. I couldn't get any words out, though. I just nodded. She called me Spank. I didn't even think she knew they called me that. Actually, I don't think she has ever called me Billy Ray, either.

I usually head to history class with Bobby as fast as we can go so we can get a quick look at the Mrs. Riley, the good-looking French teacher who stands out in front of her classroom the first few minutes of the break. I keep trying to determine her weight class, which I know is a bad habit of mine. But as a wrestler, I'm just too used to looking at people that way. At least I keep my estimations to myself.

So when Bobby saw I was walking with Laurie, he looked at me as if I had just kicked him in the mouth. He took a few steps with us but then got the hint.

"Don't want to put you on the spot, Spank," Laurie said. "But I broke up with Kelly over the weekend and I need a date to the winter formal a week from Saturday since I'm on the court. Would you go with me? If you would, I could meet you there or my dad could pick you up and take us."

First things first. I should probably mention Kelly. The Kelly Carson. He is a linebacker on the football team and a pitcher on the baseball team and a guy who probably makes some girls walk into each other when he comes down the hall. Some say he looks like that actor Chris Hemsworth who has fought whales and big mythological creatures in the movies. Kelly is a junior and drives a yellow 2019 Mustang, which I guess is a big deal out in the parking lot. Especially when you compare it to my Trek mountain bike.

Enough about him. Back to Laurie Middlebrook and mmmmmmeeee. And that's how I pretty much answered her.

"Mmmmmeeeee?"

She laughed as we headed down the hallway, her sort of leading the way since I didn't know where we were going.

"I'm sorry," she continued. "Maybe you already have a date."

I didn't tell her that I've never been on a date in my life.

"Not at this time," I said and realized that was a silly reply.

She laughed again.

"Then say yes. You've always been such a nice guy. I even remember when you retrieved my papers back in seventh grade when the wind blew them out of my hand at the bus stop. How's that for a memory? I don't want to pressure you, but I think we would have fun."

So I got out a yes before I stammered, "Laurie, I need to tell you that there may be a vicious rumor that was started by someone today that I may have a little bit of a crush on you."

"I may have heard something like that," she said as she walked into her biology class. "But I always sort of knew you did. And that made it a little easier for me to think of you for the dance."

With that, she gave me a little wave while I just stood there in the hallway like one of those Walking Dead zombies. Mrs. Riley walked by me and I didn't even notice her.

CHAPTER 4

I won't go into all my dealings with Wheat after school but you can bet I didn't hit her in the arm like Big Jim Guffie did to his crazy sister. She told me she hadn't told Laurie about my crush on her and I believed her. We let it drop. We had a meet to get ready for. I didn't even tell her about my big winter formal news.

I was still about a pound heavy when Ric drove us back to school after we did our homework up in our room and passed on supper. I knew a couple of miles around the gym in a sweat suit would take at least a pound off.

At the weigh-in, we found out that our 120-pounder, Benny Goodchild, had the flu. Coach Mathews decided to jump me up to that spot on the varsity since we don't have another wrestler at that weight. Great, I thought. All that sweating for nothing.

"You're every bit as good as Benny," Wheat told me.

"Yeah, but he's only won four matches this year — and one was a forfeit," I said.

While we warmed up in the gym, I tried to figure out who the Adams' 120-pounder was. I finally realized he was the squatty little dude, hardly five-foot-even and built something like a fireplug. That's usually not the kind of opponent you want in wrestling.

But I guess one good thing about wrestling is that you only go up against people who weight the same as you. When they say, "Pick on somebody your own size," wrestling lets that happen. Or in my case, you can sometimes say, "Get picked on by somebody your own size."

When Wheat looked over at my opponent, she said, "Who shaved that little gorilla?"

"Thanks for the encouragement," I said, and then almost gagged. "Geez, Wheat, you got enough of that Midnight Breeze on?"

"Just applied it," she said. "I'm sure it will tone down in a few minutes."

She barely had a few minutes. Billy Thurston got flopped on his back in the first 20 seconds of his 106-pound match and was pinned in less than a minute. Then he headed for the drinking fountain, of course, as if he had just been through some long ordeal.

Then the Adams 113-pounder, a guy named Terry Dibbits, stared at Wheat like that big Russian guy in Creed 2 during their handshake. (Ric has made us watch that movie about a dozen times.) I don't know if he was smelling anything at all but his own hormones — do hormones let out a smell?— but I noticed that the official said a few words to Wheat and chuckled.

Wheat ended up having to come back from a 5-3 deficit to win with a pin late in the third period. Dibbits wouldn't shake her hand afterwards and was escorted back to his team by the official. There was some boos from the crowd. I looked over at my parents in the stands and Ric just shrugged before giving me a thumbs-up.

I don't mind Ric being at meets. Mom is a different story. She knows absolutely nothing about wrestling but it doesn't keep her from shouting out encouragements and some really dumb stuff. Lake may know more than she does. He can say "win" and "pin," mainly for Wheat. He has not yet added "trounced" to his vocabulary, which is probably a good thing for me.

So it was my turn. Magilla Gorilla, real name "Something" Spenser, quickly slammed my pretty face down on the mat and then I spent the whole first period underneath him, barely avoiding a pin. But then about halfway through the second period, he seemed to hit the wall. By the third period, I was in control and actually won the match, 10-8. First and maybe last varsity win.

Wheat grabbed me when I came off the mat and gave me a big hug and then the rest of the team sort of enveloped me. Nice feeling. When we broke, I could hear my mom yelling my name and I noticed that I smelled a little like Midnight Breeze myself after Wheat's embrace.

I knew my left eye was stinging from the first-period takedown. By the time I got home, I saw I had the makings of a pretty impressive black eye.

"You not only win but now you get to look tough as well," Wheat giggled.

Mom was all upset by it but Ric thought it was pretty neat, too. I think they had a few words later about their difference of opinions. Mom and I are pretty protective of one another. We got that way when we it was just her and me those four years after my real dad died. She has let Ric take over that protective role a little, but I know she still has some mama bear in her if anyone crosses me. I think our whole family is like that now.

But back to my black eye. It was fine with me. I guess it showed that I was doing something. I was just glad that Magilla hadn't broken my nose when he took me down.

Later when Wheat and I got in bed, I asked again about her perfume.

"I used enough, I guess, because the official smelled it," she said. "He thought that was funny. But Dibbits, he didn't say anything. He can't stand losing to me. I can understand that to a point. I've barely beaten him twice so far this year. But not shaking hands? That's pretty bad."

"Ric said he saw Dibbits' dad really getting on him out in the hallway, not about the poor sportsmanship but about losing to me," she continued. "I feel a little sorry for him."

I didn't. I know what it's like getting beat by a girl, too, and all you can do is suck it up and not worry about it if you did your best. I started to tell Wheat about Laurie asking me to the winter formal but she seemed like she was done talking. That was okay with me. I didn't think she would mind, but I'll be the first to admit that I haven't completely figured out girls yet, Wheat included.

CHAPTER 5

Next morning in Big Jim's car, Sally looked back at me and said, "Nice shiner, Little Man. Did Kelly Carson give you that?"

"He got it wrestling while winning a big match, creep," said Big Jim, who also isn't very original with his insults. "And why would some jerk like Carson have anything to do with the Spank?"

"Seems he stole his girl," Sally said. "Little Man is taking Laurie Middlebrook to the winter formal."

"How do you know that?" I almost shouted while not wanting to look Wheat's way.

"Kelly told me last night when he called up and we talked about maybe going to the dance together. We're buds from way back. But I would watch my step if I were you. He seems to still have some feelings for Miss Middlebrook."

"Tell Carson that me and the whole wrestling team would be visiting him if he touches the Spank," Big Jim said. "And Wheat could probably handle Carson herself."

We got out of the car and Sally grabbed me by my coat again, acting as if she was going to plant another big one on me. I was going to be very okay with it. But then she pushed me away.

"Don't want to put you in double trouble with Kelly," she said and wiggled off like she was the Queen of the Nile or something.

Now I had to face Wheat. She looked more hurt than angry.

"When were you going to tell me about you and Laurie Middlebrook?" she asked. "Isn't that what best friends tell each other?"

"I was going to say something today at some point," I said. "Look, I'm sorry, Wheat. Wrestling was kind of the big thing last night. And I feel a little weird about the whole thing anyway. It's my very first date ever and I thought you might make fun of me. As far as Laurie goes, I'm sure I'm just a temporary stop-gap in between her big-time boyfriends."

Then Wheat's mood really changed.

"That's what really ticks me off about you, Spank. You always sell yourself short. Just because you're a dinky little person like me doesn't mean you aren't one of the best guys around. And you have your share of good looks, thanks to Mom. Laurie Middlebrook has herself a real date – not some overgrown Ken doll who thinks he has to go around acting tough all the time. So quit with the inferiority complex."

She stormed off. It was the second day in a row we didn't walk into school together. Inferiority complex? Why shouldn't I have an inferiority complex when I have to look up to three-fourths of the girls in my class and my sister can kick my butt any time she wants?

But then I started thinking. In the last 24 hours, I got a knock-your-socks-off kiss from Sally Guffie, a date proposal from the girl of my dreams and a threat of sorts from one of the school's Mr. Cools, Kelly Carson. Maybe I really was destined to become a Big Man on Campus, the "big" a figurative term, of course. I started to feel a little smug as I walked to my locker.

That smile faded pretty quickly, though. Of all people to meet in the hall but Kelly Carson himself and a couple of his football buddies. They may have even been waiting for me.

"Hey, Rogers!" he yelled.

Remember, Rogers is my last name. No Spank from him.

"Nice shiner. Who gave you that? Probably that little spitfire of a sister of yours, right?"

I didn't think he would believe me if I said it was from a guy who resembled Magilla Gorilla and so I said, "I can't remember if it was Sally Guffie or Laurie Middlebrook," before I could stop myself.

I guess I haven't told you yet that even though I look like a wimp and partly am one, I still can be a bit of smart aleck. That's probably not a good combination. Where was Sally Guffie when I needed her? One of her kisses might turn me into a frog so I could hop away.

Kelly's cocky smile had quickly faded and he picked me up and banged me into the lockers, not that hard, but hard enough to make a pretty loud clanging noise. Yeah, I guess he still had some feelings for Laurie, like Sally had said.

But before I could find out how much feelings, Mrs. Riley (did I tell you she was the Miss Delaware second runner-up while she was in college?) came out of her room and yelled at Kelly to put me down. He did so immediately. I think every guy in school has a crush on her, even the great Kelly Carson.

Mrs. Riley looked at me and seemed alarmed when she saw my blossoming black eye.

"Kelly Carson, did you do that to that young man?"

He shook his head while I said, "It's an old one, Mrs. Riley. Kelly was just seeing how many inches I have to grow before I can look him in the eye."

Kelly even grinned at that one and sort of wiped off my shoulders like something was on them. I don't think Kelly is that bad of a guy and was just showing off a little for his two buddies. But he does apparently think he's God's gift to women, which may be partly true. I noticed that even Mrs. Riley called him by name and referred to me as "that young man." Oh, well, 113-pound wrestlers with a 1-0 varsity record don't get the same notice as golden-boy football and baseball heroes.

As Kelly walked up to apologize to Mrs. Riley – not sure why he was apologizing to her – he looked over his shoulder and said, "Later, shrimp."

Trying to keep with the water creature theme, I called back, "Later, Great White," and his two friends thought that was hilarious.

Let me say this: I don't think there is anything funny about bullying. But when you grow up a shrimp, you sort of learn to deal with some of it. I always figure what goes around comes around and I do have my limits on what I will take, especially when it comes to someone else getting bullied. It's a hard subject to talk about. I'll let it go for now. But I decided Kelly wasn't going to get any more free passes from me. I really did. Do I sound scary?

I did get a lot of looks all morning because of my black eye. I think I liked the attention. Black eyes don't really hurt after a while and I guess I felt it made me look tough even though it meant somebody else gave it to me. "You should see the other guy," I said to a few gawkers.

"Or girl," said Bobby Taylor as we walked to English class after lunch. "Wheat give you that?"

"Got it last night while winning a varsity match," I said rather proudly. "You should see the other... I guess you heard that one."

"About a half dozen times in the last 30 seconds," Bobby said. "And what's with Laurie Middlebrook and you? You look about 20 thousand leagues over your head."

Funny, I thought. One of the kids in our class had just given a book report on Jules Verne's Twenty Thousand Leagues Under the Sea. Bobby had incorporated it into a conversation. He's not usually that quick-witted. I ignored his joke, though.

"She asked me to the winter formal. And, yeah, you're right. I'm way over my head."

I started getting Hummingbird Heart as we walked into class. I couldn't wait for Laurie to take a gander at my black eye. And when she looked up at me, her smile suddenly turned to a look of concern.

"Oh, wow, Spank, that looks really painful. What happened to you?"

"Don't worry," I smiled. "I won. You should see the other guy. Pretty much a drubbing — ha, ha."

Apparently, that was the wrong thing to say. She seemed to stare right through me.

"I'm not really into tough guys," she finally said. "I didn't know you fashioned yourself one. To be honest, that's one of the reasons I broke up with Kelly. I'm a sports fan — love the Cubs and Notre Dame — but I get really tired of the macho stuff that some of the guys think they have to show to impress people."

I gulped and quickly changed gears.

"I'm not tough at all," I almost whined. "I got it in a wrestling match and I'm really not very good. My sister can even beat me — badly. You could probably even beat me up. I just wrestle to stay in shape and keep my girlish figure."

She finally smiled a little.

"I forgot that you wrestled. My dad was a wrestler in high school. Or so he says. You can't always believe what politicians say. Your sister can really beat you up?"

"Yep, she's a lot tougher than me."

"But you're not a wimp?"

"Kind of somewhere in between a wimp and a tough guy, I guess, but probably a little closer to a wimp. Am I still taking you to the winter formal?"

"Yes. That is unless Tom Holland returns my calls."

I started to tell her that Wheat also had a bit of a crush on the Spiderman actor but I thought that Holland was pretty friendly with Zendaya, one of those one-name super stars. Then she giggled and squeezed my bicep, which was sore like most of my muscles after my big victory.

"Ouch!" I shouted as the tardy bell rang.

Just about the whole class of mainly girls, some of them doing a little eavesdropping, laughed.

CHAPTER 6

Later at practice, Coach Mathews pulled Wheat and me aside and said that Benny Goodchild's mom had called and said that along with the flu, he had sprained his big toe pretty badly on the bed post while rushing to the bathroom to throw up.

I didn't ask if he made it to the toilet while hobbling on his bad toe, but I sort of wanted to. I know that's pretty weird. I was thinking there's nothing's worse than ...

Oops. I suddenly came back to reality when I figured why Coach had decided to share this story with us. "At least for the near future, you're going to be our varsity 120-pounder, Spank," he said.

That "great" news almost made me want to find something to bang my own big toe up against. Maybe I should have been feeling bad for Benny but I was thinking only about myself.

And "Whoa!" or "Woe!" were the words that I was thinking. Those are homophones, by the way. I just learned about those and I felt both were appropriate to my current situation.

I know it's a bit of a cop-out but I was totally satisfied wrestling junior varsity behind Wheat. Now I was going to have to step out of her little shadow and probably get the stuffings beat out of me a couple of times a week.

The difference between most 120-pound wrestlers and 113-pound wrestlers is about seven pounds of muscle, if you get my drift. But, hey, I would be getting a chance to win a varsity letter, maybe coming with a few dislocated body parts.

"Good stuff," Wheat said before she headed to the girls' locker room to change into her wrestling togs. "Now you can bulk up and eat anything you want. I'm kind of jealous."

"Then why don't you wrestle 120 and I'll take your 113 spot?" I said. "It seems only fair since you're better than me."

"You're probably right," she said, "but …"

She didn't finish and so I did it for her. "But you have a better chance of being a state champ at 113. That's what I want, too, Wheat. You a state champ. I just don't want us to be known as the Champ and Chump Siblings."

"Spank, I think you're going to be a lot better than you think. In fact, once you get out from behind me, I think you may flourish. I've never said this before but I don't think you quite try your best against me. You hold back a little whether you know it or not. You put up a good fight but I think you have more. You showed it last night."

"Whatever you say, Wheat," I said half-heartedly.

But I thought about what she said as we warmed up. Maybe I was holding back a little. Maybe I was better than I thought I was. And then I went out and worked with Doug Littlejohn, a junior varsity wrestler at 126 pounds. He whipped me good in some takedown drills and seemed to like it a little too much. He's a bit of a knucklehead, always bragging about this or that. He's still a teammate, though.

With moving up a weight class, I was going to be paired with him more in practice. Then after he got done with me, Wheat kicked my butt a few times. By then, I was barely able to handle Tommy the Torso.

I was dragging that night as we sat down to the dinner table. Then I smiled when I remembered I could eat all I wanted. Of all nights for Mom to plop down a big dish of chicken chow mein, not one of my favorites. I call it "chicken bowel pain" when she is out of earshot.

"By the way," Mom said to me after our family prayer. "A Laurie Meadowbrook phoned and asked that you return her call tonight."

"Middlebrook, Mom," Wheat piped up. "Laurie Middlebrook. The mayor's daughter, the beauty queen type, and Spank's new flame."

I decided to get the humiliation over with.

"I guess I'm going to the winter formal with her," I said, my voice becoming a little shaky.

My mom squealed — actually squealed. Gosh, how embarrassing. Ric just nodded his head with a big smile on his face. Wheat looked like she was going to burst out laughing. Lake was the only one who didn't seem obligated for some comical reaction, concentrating on making a mess out of his apple sauce.

"When were you going to tell us this big news?" Mom asked.

"It's not big news, Mom," I said. "It's just a date. That's all."

"Your first date, though, honey," she said. "That's very big. I know you probably don't believe this, but you will never forget your first date."

Especially if the time leading up to it was going to get any worse, I thought.

"How are you going to get to this event?" Ric asked. "Is she light enough that she can sit up on your handlebars or can I help you out?"

"Laurie said her dad would drive us," I said as all this talk started to make my belly buck a little.

"Wow, that's pretty impressive," Mom added. "You get the mayor as a chauffeur. Maybe your dad can at least give you a police escort in his squad car."

I didn't laugh but Mom can actually be pretty funny. When it was just her and me that four years after my real dad died, she tried to keep things positive as much as she could. We were always joking around and she had some great stories to share about her kindergartners. She also would sing along with all the popular songs on the car radio, making me join in. I look back now and realize how hard that must have been for her to keep our spirits up.

When she and Ric first got married, I'm not sure Mom thought it was that good of an idea for me to wrestle and maybe get hurt. She was a little baffled about Wheat wresting anyway.

"She wrestles boys?" I remember her saying to Ric when I wasn't quite out of earshot. "Whatever for?"

She adjusted, though. She always has. She may be a little overprotective but I couldn't think of a better Mom. For four years, she was both my Mom and Dad. She would take me to superhero movies that I know she really didn't like and even tried to play pitch-and-catch with me although she took one of my throws off her glove and into her face. It bruised up pretty good. She was back at it the next day with me, though. She's tough. I just don't like her squealing when she hears something about me she likes.

But Mom didn't really react when Wheat let go with the other big news. "Spank is going to stay at varsity at 120 pounds. Bennie Goodchild sprained his big toe while running to the bathroom to puke."

To be honest, that's what I felt like doing as Ric cheered that new announcement — the part about me staying at varsity, I think, not Bennie spraining his toe. What little I ate of the "chicken bowel pain" wasn't settling in so well. The thought of my big date and then wrestling varsity against guys bigger than me suddenly made me feel like my stomach contents weren't all that safe. I held back a gag.

"May I be excused?" I barely got out.

"You've only eaten half your meal and now you can eat all you want," Mom said.

"Well, I'm about ready to do my Bennie Goodchild impersonation, hopefully without spraining my toe," I said.

Everybody seemed a little shocked but Mom who said, "Go, go."

I hit the downstairs half bathroom at a full run, but all I could manage was a couple of weak dry heaves. I think it was more nerves stuck in my throat than anything else. By that time, Ric had knocked on the bathroom door and walked on in.

"You okay, bud?" he asked.

"Yep."

"Hey, a lot on your plate right now and I don't mean the chicken chow mein. Never tell your Mom this but it's not my favorite, either."

"I'll be fine," I said more confidently than I was really feeling.

Ric patted my shoulder and paused like he had something to say. But then he left me alone, while I wondered if I could eat a couple of bowls of Cheerios before bed without hurting Mom's feelings.

I decided that a little air would do me good and walked outside onto our front porch. It was probably 30 degrees, not bad for a late January night. I didn't even bother with a coat. Wrestling at 120 pounds and weighing 113 — maybe more like 112 after passing on most of my supper — I didn't have any reason to do a lot of sweating.

But before I knew it, my legs just started jogging. I've already told you that's what a lot of wrestlers do anytime there's some open space in front of them. I started circling our block out in the street because some of our neighbors hadn't done a very good job of keeping the snow off their sidewalks. By the time I had finished my first lap, Wheat was out in front of our house waiting for me.

She doesn't like walking or running by the funeral home alone when it's dark. She doesn't talk about it much but I know it spooks her a little, especially when we know a body is inside. It doesn't bother me at all, but the big viewing room is on our house's side — not 50 feet from our second-floor bedroom window. I think that might be another reason Wheat doesn't mind sharing a room with me. Maybe the main reason.

She looked a little like a ghost herself with a white hoodie pulled tight around her face.

"I could use a little run to work off some of that meal, too," she said as she joined me.

It's about 600 yards around our block and we didn't say a word on my second lap.

Then about halfway through the third lap, Wheat finally said, "Don't keep your lady waiting too long, Spank."

I ignored her until we were just starting our fourth lap.

"I don't want you listening in," I said and then picked up the pace, scooting by Mr. Saunders who was out walking his mean little Boston terrier, Bootsie.

Bootsie may be the only dog I dislike in the whole world and, of course, he made a lunge at me.

Mr. Saunders jerked him back and Wheat fell right over Bootsie who let out a yelp. I really took off then. I rounded the second corner and headed down Elm Street — which is our backstretch. After another turn and with about 100 yards to go, I heard Wheat coming, huffing and puffing more than you would have thought a skinny little girl could. She passed me in a dead sprint just a couple of feet *after* our front walkway, which we consider our finish line.

"Beat ya," I gasped.

"Yeah, well I had to untangle myself from that little mutt Bootsie and then listen to Mr. Saunders yell at me for scaring him half to death. And that it was disrespectful to be playing — like we were playing — in front of a funeral home," she said between heavy breaths. "I'd like to hit that Bootsie with a shovel and stick him in a little cardboard casket outside the funeral home with a note that says to bury him deep."

We agreed on that. Actually, I was smiling. I had beaten Wheat in a race — a rarity — and I also didn't need to go into our house and weigh myself after a run. "I'm ready for my big call now."

"You go, girl," Wheat said.

"You got it, little brother," I replied.

CHAPTER 7

Inside, Lake was waddling along with his diaper drooping.

"Barf, barf, barf," he said while grinning at me.

I looked at Wheat as she came in the door behind me.

"You teach him that?" I asked.

"No, you did," she said. "I just told him the word that described what you were doing."

I playfully threw a punch at her and stopped it two inches from her nose. She, in turn, started a kick that came about that close to my privates.

"Too bad those kind of moves can't be used in wrestling," she said as she picked up Lake to see if he had any leakage.

"When you grow up, you'll probably be an ultimate fighter with a name like Scorch and you can kick and bite to your heart's content," I said.

"Scorch? I was thinking a little more mythological like Circe or Electra," she said.

"Stay out of our room for a while, Medusa. I need a little privacy for my big call."

"Oooh, you stink," she said.

I immediately smelled my right armpit until I realized that she was talking about Lake. For some reason, I was thinking I better be at my best before my call. But then Laurie wasn't going to be able to see me, let alone smell me. I guess I was just a little jittery.

So I headed up to our room to use the cell phone that Wheat and I share. We mainly have it for emergencies and it usually stays in Wheat's backpack. I know, I know, kids our age are supposed to be on their phones all the time. We just mainly talk to each other face to face. That usually seems good enough. I guess we're mavericks that way. Or nerds.

Yeah, I was nervous. My hands were already sweating even though I'd just come inside from the cold. Hey, Laurie Middlebrook wanted me to call her. Who knows, maybe she had come to her senses and was going to cancel our date.

Mom had written down her number on a piece of paper and her 7s and 9s always look a lot alike. Were there two 9s in Laurie's number or two 7s or one of each? I tried the 7s first, considering them lucky, and Laurie did indeed answer — on the second ring.

"Hello," she said in a way that her one word could never be spoken any sweeter.

Nothing came out of my mouth for a few seconds. Then I sounded (wouldn't you know it?) like a frog croaking when I finally could say, "Hi Laurie, this is Billy Ray ... or Spanky ... or anything else you want to call me — like Mr. Goofy with the way I probably sound right now."

"I know all of you," she said. "But I really like Spanky."

"You do?" I said before I realized she was just talking about my nickname and not me, myself and I.

She laughed.

"I like your name and you're pretty likable, too. But what do I hear about you and Sally Guffie? The rumor is that you and her were putting on a pretty good show out in the parking lot a couple of days ago."

"I was not responsible for any of that," I said, horror in my voice." An innocent victim. I ride to school with her brother and she's the other passenger with me and my sister. She frightens me. And it was only one kiss forced upon me and I quickly wiped it off."

I waited for a reaction. Laurie chuckled.

"You're a funny guy, Spank."

"Only if you want me to be," I said.

"I only want you to be yourself," she said in a more serious tone. "Actually, I would like to get to know you a little better before the dance since that's supposed to be one of those big deals in the lives of teenagers. I wondered if you would meet me for a Coke. Because I'm on the court, there's a few extra things we have to do. Are you free tomorrow evening? We could meet at Mug and Munchies."

"I could do that," I said, smacking my head with my free hand to keep myself from fainting.

"And why don't you bring your sister Tanda if she would like to come. I've really never been around her much and would like to get to know her, too."

Hmmm, I didn't see that coming.

"Sort of like a chaperone," I said with a little disappointment probably coming through in my voice.

"No, no," she said. "I figure I'll learn more about you from her than I will from you. I also figure she could cut down in any awkwardness or lapses in the conversation. That can happen on first dates. Or maybe I should call it a pre-date. By the way, why didn't you FaceTime me?"

I had to tell her the truth.

"I don't know how," I said. "Wheat usually has the phone. I think she might know how."

"Well, maybe I could show you how sometime. And Spank? Sally Guffie? You'll have to work a lot harder for a kiss from me, okay?"

"Okay," I answered and then she hung up with a quick "Bye."

That "Bye" was even better than her "Hello," if you can believe that. When I watch old movies with Ric, people rarely say "Goodbye" or "Bye" or "Drop Dead, Fred" at the end of their calls.

They just hang up. I don't like that. I think it tells you a lot about a person by the way he or she ends a conversation. I was thinking about writing somebody like Steven Spielberg or Tom Hanks in Hollywood about that. I think I have a good point here.

Anyway, I went up and took a cold shower after Laurie's hello, bye, and everything in between. I never quite understood why people said they needed to take a cold shower in the movies and in books. Now I think I know. I eventually let the water warm up so I could stay in there a little longer. I didn't think I was ready to talk to Wheat about all this.

Finally, Ric knocked on the bathroom door and told me I didn't need to use up all the hot water.

When I walked into our room with a towel on, Wheat said, "Hey, Mr. Prune."

I decided to get it over with.

"Okay. The call went well, I think. I'm meeting Laurie for a Coke tomorrow night at Mug and Munchies. And she wants you to come, too. Got a problem with that?"

"Wow," she said. "Is that a half of a double-date or something?

"Nope, a pre-date. You're there because she would like to meet you and for you to fill in the conversation gaps."

"Yeah, yeah, I can do that," she said, sounding almost excited.

Then the subject dropped, thankfully. I did some biology homework, fought a little in "Clash of the Clans" on my computer (it's rare I have the time to do that during wrestling season) and watched a half hour of "Young Sheldon" on TV. He's a nerd like me, but is too smart to know it.

———

Thank goodness the next day — Thursday — was back to normal. Sally Guffie pretty much ignored me in her brother's car, Kelly Carson gave me a "thumbs down" sign when I sort of skated by him while he was talking up some girl at her locker and Laurie Middlebrook gave me a nice smile and sweet hello in English class and little else. Oh, yeah, and Wheat kicked my butt at practice, although I do believe she is right — I might be getting a little better.

I did have to practice some with Dion Borden, our 126-pound varsity guy and one of our senior captains. He's good and takes wrestling just as seriously as Wheat. He can handle her because of the size difference but she can sometimes give him a pretty good battle when they square off at practice. He probably makes Wheat a better wrestler, which I probably do not.

"You wearing perfume, too?" he asked me before we worked on our escape moves.

I don't usually get too riled up, but that did bug me a little. I'm not totally sure why. I busted out of a chicken-wing hold he had on me and danced around a little like Muhammed Ali for a couple of seconds. We went at it pretty good the rest of the session. Yeah, he kicked my butt but I did better than I would have expected. Later, I pretty much held my own against Doug Littlejohn, Dion's understudy.

"Pretty good, Spank," Dion said later on when we worked on our reverse moves. "Not sure why you didn't move up to 120 in the first place. You've always been better than Benny."

I just nodded but, boy, did that make my chest puff out a little. Okay, I'm not sure if my chest really puffed out but I like that expression. Dion is one of our leaders, after all, and a guy who is probably going places. I like that expression, too.

When Big Jim dropped us off at home, I was ready to do a lot of eating. Heck, if I was going to be wrestling 120 pounds, I might as well try to weigh 120 pounds. Mom was serving spaghetti and meatballs and that's one of my favorite meals. I filled my plate twice and Ric and Mom just looked at me.

"Settle down, bro," Wheat said as she stuck a couple of meatballs on a small salad and then weighed them. "You're wrestling 120, not 132. Besides, you don't want to be burping the whole time you're sitting beside Laurie Middlebrook tonight."

"You're sitting beside her," I said. "I'm scooting in across from her."

"Whoa," Ric said. "You're going tonight, too, Wheat?"

"Whoa," Lake mimicked.

"Yep, the chaperone. Can I borrow your taser, Dad, just in case Spank acts inappropriately?"

"For goodness sakes," Mom chimed in. "Is anything going to happen that should concern me?"

"Noooo," I said.

"Whoa," Lake added.

CHAPTER 8

We ended up walking the half mile to Mug and Munchies. Wheat wanted to jog but I nixed that. I didn't want Laurie to see us looking like we couldn't wait to get there.

Mug and Munchies is on the corner of Elm and Barton streets and is made to look like one of those old-time soda shops, according to Mom. Laurie Middlebrook was in her dad's car outside the hangout.

Mr. Middlebrook rolled down his window and started to get out of his big black Lincoln with Laurie but she quickly vetoed that.

"That's Spanky and Tanda, Dad. You can talk them up another time. Just do your wave. They're too young to vote for you anyway."

He smiled at us out his window and said, "I'll be back in an hour, sweetie. Have fun."

We pretty much did. Yeah, it was a little awkward at first, especially when it came to the seating arrangements. I had predicted that. Wheat scooted in on one side of the booth and I started to follow her when she stuck her foot out across the seat. Laurie had already sat down on the other side and I took the hint from Wheat and moved in beside Laurie. Yeah, that had been Wheat's plan all along.

But I was glad Wheat was there. She actually said nice things about me, at least most of the time, and made Laurie laugh a lot. I liked her laugh. We found out that she had recently got fed up with a couple of her girlfriends who she thought put too much emphasis on clothes and other material things. She said she was hoping to expand her social circle, which made me wonder why she was hanging out with a square like me. Get it — square, circle? I kept that to myself.

She seemed really curious about our wrestling, especially about Wheat's. But then Wheat mentioned that we took ball room dancing lessons on Monday nights. I guess I haven't said anything about that yet, have I?

Laurie almost coughed part of her Coke out her nose when Wheat told her how I had accidentally put my hand on Jessica Lercher's bottom when she was showing me the foxtrot last winter. Jessica was a senior at Clay then and the reigning homecoming queen. She's still an assistant teacher at our dance classes while going to Saint Mary's College. She is big-time beautiful, probably in Sally Guffie's weight class and about three inches taller than I am. So my hand came about level with her bottom and I was so nervous that I didn't even know it was there.

Jessica gave me a little open-handed tap on my cheek — more out of ballroom formality than anger, I think — as she jerked my hand away with her other hand. I later got her a glass of punch and she said, "Thanks, young man."

Not sure I liked being called young man by an 18-year-old, but bottom line — ha, ha — I figured that made us somewhat even.

"So Spank, am I going to have a hard time staying up with you on the dance floor at the winter formal?" Laurie asked.

"Only if I bruise your toes too much by stepping on them," I answered. "I am not all that thrilled about the lessons. Don't like them very much. In fact, Wheat owes me big time for her even being in this year's class."

Which was true. We both took ball room dancing the previous year because Ric had this idea that it might help our coordination and fluid motion. Mom was all in because she thought it might bring up our sophistication level. They both might have been right — a little — but not enough for me to take it a second year even though I was pretty good at it, if I do say so myself.

So my parents gave me a pass even though Wheat was all excited about doing another year. The trouble was that Mom forgot to sign up Wheat by the deadline and they had more girls than boys in the class. So the instructor, Mrs. Gray, said if I would go again and bring a friend, Wheat could attend. I think I was one of Mrs. Gray's favorites since I did pick up the moves pretty quickly, smiled like I was having a good time and didn't act like an idiot around the punch bowl.

Not a great deal for me, even though I was going to get five bucks a session for being some sort of junior assistant instructor. It took my parents a lot longer into talking me into this compromise than it took me to convince Bobby Taylor to go for another year. He won't admit it, but I know he is a little sweet on Wheat and he liked the fact that we would be carpooling again.

Laurie obviously liked hearing all of this and so I started liking her even more.

"Do you guys ever worry about cauliflower ears in wrestling?" she asked out of the blue.

"Sure," Wheat said. "I worry about giving them to Spank."

We all laughed — the girls a little louder than me.

Wheat did say that we wore headgear, which wasn't all that great for making her hair look nice.

"Do you ever worry about beating boys and hurting their feelings?" she asked Wheat. "And do you mind if I call you Tanda? I think that's too pretty of a name to waste it."

"Sure," Wheat or Tanda said. "I'm getting a little tired of Wheat anyway."

I did not know that. But then I found something else that surprised me even more.

"Yeah, it does bother me a little how the boys feel after I beat them," Wheat continued. "I know it shouldn't. And when I'm out on the mat, I'm certainly not thinking that way. I want to win. I want to get a pin. But afterwards, I'll sometimes watch a guy who I just beat and see how he's taking it. I hate to see it if his parents — or worse yet, a girlfriend — have to console him. I feel a little bad for him."

"Are you like that with Spank, too?" Laurie asked, while looking right at me.

"Naaaa," she said. "He won't admit it, especially to himself, but he's getting better and better. But he needs to be reminded now and then how hard it is to be really good at wrestling and I'm there to remind him. Besides, he needs a little humbling now that you asked him to the winter formal."

I know I turned beet red at that point. I could have killed Wheat, who was looking very pleased with herself.

Then I felt Laurie put her hand in mine and say, "Show me some of your dance moves, Spank, so I can see if I need to be practicing. Just don't grab me like you did Jessica Lercher."

I looked around the place and besides the one waitress, Jenny, there were only a trio of middle school girls and Bobby Brayton and Ellie Robistelli, two seniors at our school who were studying in their booth. They both live over on Elm Street behind us and are supposed to be competing against each other for valedictorian honors in their class. They are always nice.

I guessed we wouldn't make too much of a scene, but the music was all wrong for waltzing since Katy Perry was on the juke box singing, "Swish, Swish." It didn't seem to matter to Laurie who was sort of scooting me out of the booth.

"Hey, Spank, if you're not interested, I bet Wheat would show me," Laurie said.

I shook my head and stood up. I put my hand around Laurie's back like I knew what I was doing, probably making all those stinking dancing sessions worthwhile. And off we went. After two years of this stuff, I can put on a pretty good imitation of that guy who's always showing his bare chest in Dancing With the Stars. And even though my hands started getting sweaty, we probably looked pretty good. Bobby and Ellie even stopped studying and gave us a little clap.

I looked over at Wheat who flashed a smile back at us. And then she suddenly frowned. A second later, I felt a hard hand on my shoulder that turned me around. And there I was, looking at none other than Kelly Carson who was wearing his highly-decorated letter jacket along with a smile right out of a stack of jokers. Two of his buddies, Tom Chester and Boyd Eli, were behind him looking like Beavis and Butthead.

I didn't move. But Laurie did.

She moved in between us and said, "This is a private dance, buddy. Leave us alone. You don't figure in my free time anymore."

It all seemed to be becoming a little Karate Kiddish — you know that early scene on the beach when the bully busts the radio and then wails on Daniel, one of my all-time movie heroes. Ric loves that "The Karate Kid." Like I said, he loves his movies — especially from the 1980s when he was growing up.

Too bad Ric wasn't around to play Mr. Miyagi.

When Kelly tried to kiss Laurie, I was still standing flat-footed, a little shocked by the whole scene. Laurie was finally able to pull away and tried to slap him but missed. That's when my body seemed to wake up. I moved forward and tried to shove Kelly away only to have him push me across the room.

I fell on my butt and was a little slow getting up. And when I did, I saw the craziest of sights. Wheat was on top of Kelly and riding him like a cowboy trying to brand a steer. Bobby Brayton had gotten up from his booth and was standing between them and

Heckle and Jeckle and saying that Ellie was on her cell phone calling his twin brother Billy, the toughest guy in the school.

Bobby is kind of a sissy but his brother scares the bejabbers out of everyone and that was good enough to keep this match between just Kelly and Wheat. He was trying his best to get out from under her but she had switched to what professional wrestlers would call a camel clutch, bending his head back.

Kelly started screaming bloody murder and Tony the Cook, who has a Marine tattoo on his right forearm, finally came out of the kitchen and around the counter.

"All over," he said. "If I were you, buddy, I'd quit before you look even more like a laughing stock than you already do."

Wheat let Kelly go. But when he started to get up, he swept his legs out and tripped Wheat. She went down on her bottom and Kelly stood up above her like he was some kind of conquering hero or something. Then Laurie jumped on his back but he bucked her off.

And that's when it happened. Before I knew what I was doing, my right hand was suddenly in a fist. Have you ever seen the first "Back to the Future" movie when Marty McFly's goofy dad sort of goes into a trance as a teen-ager and decks the bully Biff? I think I was having that same kind of out-of-body experience.

Honestly, I've never hit anybody with my fist in my life. And my record is still clean. I just couldn't talk my arm into coming forward and throwing a punch. But I had momentum going toward Kelly and when I tripped on some mushy fries that had been knocked on the floor, I tumbled into him — hard. My noggin, in headbutt position, smashed into his jaw, a glass jaw evidently. That was not my plan but I'm going to say it: It felt pretty darn good. Kelly went down and one of his buddies then seemed to be on me.

By the time the dust settled, Billy Brayton and the mayor were coming in the door about the same time and Ric was pulling up in a squad car. I'm not sure who called him. Maybe Ellie after she called Billy. Or the waitress Jenny who used to live down the street from us.

I think a few threats were tossed out but Billy and Bobby Brayton were standing like sentinels over Wheat and me while Tony the Cook and then Ric helped Kelly, his face a little ashen, and his buddies on their way.

The mayor put his hand on his daughter's shoulder — harder than I did when we started our dance but not as hard as Kelly had grabbed her — and escorted her out. But before they got out the door, she broke loose and came back and kissed me on the cheek.

Ribbit! I wanted to pinch myself to see if I had become a frog or a prince.

"I didn't think you liked roughhousing," I said, not liking it much myself.

"Your actions were pure chivalrous," she said as she caught up with her dad, who was staring at me as if I were that greasy guy from the movie, "The Breakfast Club." I made a note to look up chivalrous in the dictionary when I got home just to make sure I had it right.

I got the feeling that some of the onlookers thought I had decked Kelly, Laurie included. I wasn't going to worry about that. You do what you have to do, even if it's by accident.

As Wheat and I climbed into the back of Ric's car, he looked back at us and said, "You mind telling me what went on in there?"

"Mr. Big Man on Campus found out he isn't so big after all," Wheat said. "And Spank just got himself a reputation."

"My, my, what are we going to do?" was all Ric said the rest of the way home.

Me? I was thinking that transferring schools, or maybe even states, might be a good idea.

Wheat, meanwhile, was feeling my bicep like it was some ripe avocado. She must have had not a good view of my "punch," either. And how come everyone suddenly wants to squeeze my bicep?

So I humored her.

"Watch it," I whispered. "I might be on a roll."

And then my Hummingbird Heart kicked in.

————

Maybe I should mention the Brayton twins now. Like I said, they live on the street behind us and their family is sort of legendary. Their granddad, who just died, played for the Chicago Cubs for a while as a backup catcher and their uncles were all good football players. Billy and Bobby have two older sisters who used to babysit us, a nice mom and their dad is the local newspaper's sport columnist, although the only sport he might have played himself was tiddlywinks.

Billy is the best athlete at our school, while Bobby is a big teddy bear. I like them both and they seem to like me. I used to take care of their paper route when their family would go on vacation and I will still walk and feed their basset hound Wrigley when they need me to.

Bobby calls me "Spankaroo" and Billy will sometimes give me a nod in the school hallway. He will probably play football for Notre Dame or someplace like that next year. Probably the only reason he isn't a state champion wrestler is that he loves his basketball, too.

I'm sure Big Jim Guffie is happy about that — not having to face Billy for the heavyweight spot. Big Jim says everyone is a little scared of Billy and that includes Kelly Carson, who is a teammate of Billy's on both the football and baseball teams.

Lucky me. I couldn't think of anything better than having a 250-pound guardian angel. And the twins apparently put out the word that I'm not supposed to be touched by Kelly or any of his friends. I can live with being 1-0 in my short-lived boxing career, although I heard through the grapevine that all bets are off when the Braytons go off to college.

Maybe by that time, I'll have eaten myself into a 170-pounder. More meatballs and less chicken choi mein would help. Hey, I'm okay as long as Kelly doesn't decide to lose 50 or 60 pounds and join the wrestling team. Fat chance — but then I would have said the same thing a week ago about me being asked to the winter formal by Laurie Middlebrook.

Anyway, the next day — Friday — was pretty tame, thank goodness, except for mom all worked up over what happened at Mug and Munchies. She wanted the details and none of us was giving her enough. I think she was more concerned about whether my date with Laurie was in jeopardy. I think she is more excited about my date than even I am — and I guess that's okay.

I didn't wash my cheek where Laurie had kissed me. At school, I even walked her to her biology class.

About the previous night, the only thing Laurie said was, "Wow, Spank, what a first date!"

I just nodded and then I said, "Was that a first date or pre-date?"

Laurie answered, "I don't know really what to call it but exhilarating."

I nodded again and I felt the hair on my neck stick up like a row of corn.

The hallway seemed to open up for us when normally people don't mind if they run me over or not. We got a lot of looks. But then I imagine that Laurie always did get a lot of looks during her pre-Spank days. I wondered what she was going to be doing on the weekend but I didn't ask. But I figured she would be with me — in my dreams — for most of it.

I thought Wheat would kid me a little about everything but she didn't. For whatever reason, I think she is pleased that I am going to the formal and that we both stood up to Kelly.

CHAPTER 9

Since we didn't have a Saturday invitational, I was looking forward to sleeping in. I had wrestled harder than ever the previous few days and I figured I deserved to get out of our morning running session. Hey, I didn't have to worry about my weight and this was one of the few weekends we didn't have some kind of competition.

But Wheat wouldn't have any of that. She grabbed me by my feet a little harder than usual and started to pull me out of bed like she didn't care if I hit the floor or not.

"You're running, too, Mr. Winter Formal," she said. "Misery loves company and I'm not going to listen to Dad's singing by myself. I really think he's got the idea that he sounds pretty good."

So after a lot of moaning on my part, the three of us were off. It had snowed about an inch the night before and Ric was occasionally doing a little sliding on my bike despite it having wide tires.

I'm not much of a night person — and I consider anything between sunset and sunrise nighttime — so I'm not usually at my best out in the dark. Wheat, meanwhile, must see like a cat. She doesn't miss anything, including any little movement around the funeral home.

And she was the first of us to notice the two guys down the block after we rounded the corner onto Gable Street. They looked like they were trying to get into a parked car. Then we heard the sound of breaking glass.

"Hey!" Ric yelled from behind us. "Police officer! Stop!"

I always wondered what he might yell when coming onto a crime scene. The two guys definitely stopped breaking into the car and took off like Olympic runners. Ric came sliding by us and Wheat and I started sprinting, too.

But then, my bike's tires slid out on Ric and he wiped out on the slick street. Wheat stopped to help him but I kept running after the guys. I'm not sure why. Maybe I was still feeling my oats after my little business with Kelly Carson. And at least one of the guys running ahead of me didn't look a whole lot bigger than me. I'll tell you one thing, though: I had Hummingbird Heart like never before.

The little guy proved to be a speedster but his burly partner was starting to falter as we all ran right down the middle of Gable. Then I heard Ric from somewhere pretty far behind me yell for all of us to stop. I guess he had gotten untangled from the bike and was trying to get back in the race. That made me feel a little braver.

The guys made a turn and ran right through a yard where a picket fence suddenly confronted them. The smaller guy was up and over it but the big guy hesitated. Then he must have heard me coming and maybe thought I was the police. He got some steam going but I was now close enough to go for the tackle.

I hit him about calf high and slid down his leg only to have his boot come off in my hands. He stayed up, hobbled off and tried to vault the fence only to cry out a dirty word when he apparently gored himself on one of the picket's top points. I don't know why but the whole scene made me think of Tom Sawyer and his paint-the-picket-fence story although I don't remember Tom using that kind of language. Huckleberry Finn probably did, though.

He then sort of half-fell, half-dove over the fence — he was no gymnast — while I was getting to my feet. He turned around and looked at me. He was dressed in black with a ski hat pulled down to his eyes and up to his chin and he was still holding some kind of long tool in his hand — probably what he broke the car window with.

"You the Keystone Cop?" he said with a gravelly voice. "Well then come on over here and arrest me, you little runt. Or at least throw me back my boot."

"No sir," I said, glad to have a four-foot high fence in between us. "I'm keeping this as evidence."

He looked like he was ready to come back after me — or the boot — when his friend yelled from a ways away for him to get going.

He patted the long rod in his free hand and said, "Maybe we'll meet again, little man."

Little man? Geez. I was starting to really hate that term.

About that time, I heard Ric yelling for me and the guy hurried out of sight between the houses while about a hundred neighborhood dogs barked and porch lights came on all over the place.

Wheat came up to me first and then Ric hobbled up, favoring one leg. He apparently had gone down on his bad football knee pretty hard when he fell off the bike. He was talking on his cell phone to the police station. I just stood there with a big brown work boot in my hand.

"Did one of them throw that at you?" Wheat asked.

Before I could come up with a smart answer, Ric grabbed me and asked if I was okay.

Then he yelled at me for doing something stupid. "You could have been seriously hurt," he bellowed. "Somebody who breaks into cars can often do other bad things — and they are often armed."

I told him that he had something long in his hand. That didn't make him any happier.

"Could you recognize him, you think?" he asked.

"All I know is that he was really big and probably really ugly. I just saw a little bit of his face. He did have a gravelly voice, though. And …"

"What?" Ric asked expectantly.

"He probably has one really cold foot," I said, holding up the boot.

Ric gave me a little clip on the back of my head and couldn't hold back a grin.

"You guys head home and get ready for school. I'm staying here and waiting for the posse. And Spank, I wouldn't go into all the details with your mom. Just say we scared away a couple of would-be burglars. And leave that boot with me."

I nodded and didn't feel it was necessary to tell Ric that there was no school on Saturday. I think he was a little rattled like all of us. He would remember soon enough what day it was. Wheat and I took off on the mile or so that we were away from home.

After about 200 yards, I said to my sister, "What's your opinion on all this?"

"I should have sprinted after them, too," she said. "And I would have tackled more than a boot."

Then she giggled and sprinted ahead of me before the snowball I quickly made missed her by about two feet to the right. That's when I noticed that my hands were sort of shaking.

CHAPTER 10

The rest of the weekend was pretty boring — but how could it be any other way after accidentally decking Kelly Carson and almost tackling a criminal? We went to the new Spiderman movie Saturday afternoon with Ric (I had popcorn and Wheat took one handful) and we caught up on our homework.

I worked on my biology project, which is how the temperature of water affects the activity of frogs. I had separated Notre and Dame into two aquariums two weeks earlier and kept Notre in water 10 degrees cooler than Dame. I don't think Notre's been all that happy about it. He certainly sits on top of his rock a lot more than Dame. I'm working on some kind of theory that hasn't exactly jumped out at me yet. Hmmm, jumped. Maybe that's what I'll do — I'll measure how far they can jump after they have been sitting in their respective temperatures.

Wheat said I should kiss each one of them and see which one dies first. I told her that she should kiss Notre and see if he turns into Prince Charming or Shrek. Then I could kiss Dame and see if she turned into a princess or stayed a frog. As you can see, I'm sort of struggling with a theme for my science project. I don't even know if Dame is a girl.

I'm also a little worried my frogs will end up being victims of our little brother's curiosity. The other day, I caught him up on my desk and throwing a couple of his little motor boats in Notre's aquarium. He said something about pee-pee water, too, before I jerked him down.

Anyway, we did go to church on Sunday morning. Wheat and I alternate in the nursery as helpers since Lake went crazy the first time Mom and Dad — yeah, I'm still working on calling Ric that more — tried to leave him there.

He doesn't mind, though, if one of us is in there with him. I don't think either Wheat or I mind, either. There are some cool little kids in there besides Lake. And we both get a little embarrassed how loud Mom sings the hymns. She's pretty good but she seems to want to drown out anybody else in the pew. I'm probably exaggerating here, but the choir leader must have noticed because she asked Mom to join the choir.

Mom said she might after Lake gets a little older. In my opinion, she needs a few hobbies. She hasn't taught kindergarten since Lake was born and I think she has too much time on her hands. She tries to get a little too involved in my and Wheat's lives if you ask me. That was okay when it was just the two of us and I was younger but it gets a little too much now. She means well but moms can be moms and she is full-time at it right now.

For example, she really pays attention to what we wear and our clothes drawers and closet at home look like we're in the Army or something. Everything has its place. Every sock has its match. Every piece of clothing is either neatly hung or folded.

I once opened a drawer that belonged to our cousin Jimmy — Uncle Mason and Aunt Lilly's youngest son — and sweat socks and dark socks were thrown in any old way. I saw a couple of candy bar wrappers in there, too. Mom might have a heart attack if one of my drawers looked like that. She might be Loosey Goosey to Ric — or Dad — but she can be a little uptight about neatness in my opinion.

Even our wrestling outfits are quickly washed and ironed when she finds them in our gym bags. So instead of bringing mine home, I've been leaving it in my locker until it really works up a good stink. If Wheat is going to use Midnight Breeze as a weapon, I might as well use good old B.O. to my advantage. Big Jim apparently has a theory about that.

Mom doesn't want us in jeans and sneakers at church, either, even though most of the kids wear them. So I have had to put on nice slacks and a pressed shirt on Sunday mornings and then a sports coat and tie on Monday nights for dance lessons. It sort of ruins the start of the week.

But with Ric's help, we finally convinced Mom that whoever works in the nursery could dress down a little since we are always on the floor playing with the toddlers and getting juice and other stuff spilled on us. And Wheat will change a diaper, which can get a little messy. I let whichever mother is in charge of the nursery do that duty.

So it's a pretty big deal to us who works in the nursery — partly because of what we can wear ... partly because of Mom's singing ... and partly because we do get a few looks in the pew. I just think that some people can't figure out our family since one week I'm sitting out with our parents and the next week, it's Wheat.

One old lady who often sits near us must not see all that well even though she wears glasses. After one service, she patted me on the arm and said she liked that I was now wearing my hair short. My hair is always short. I felt like asking her if she liked me when I had a sun-tan every other week but figured that would be rude. At least she must realize I'm a boy. I spared Wheat that story.

That reminds me of the time when Wheat and I went roller skating a few years ago. I had on a stocking cap pulled down over my ears and the guy at the counter gave me white skates just like Wheat got. I didn't think much about it until they started cutting into my toes and then noticed every other guy had on black skates.

When I took them back, saying I needed a bigger size (I guess girl size sixes aren't the same as boys size sixes), the guy gave me a bewildered look. I had taken off my stocking cap. He then gave me another pair of white ones one size bigger to wear — still girl skates. And I just took them without saying a word. I didn't do much skating after that, hanging around the snack bar. I think I'm probably confident enough now that I would say something. I hope so.

Anyway, when we got home from church, I hustled over to the funeral home and pushed a little snow off the sidewalks. Todd, the oldest of the Dixon brothers and a rangy 6-foot-5 — I just heard a sports writer use the word rangy — had called me before church and said he could also use a little help before a visitation. I thought he meant doing something like emptying all the trash receptacles and setting up some chairs, which I have done before.

But he sort of floored me when he asked if I was okay being around "people who have passed." I guess that was a more polite way of saying "being around people as dead as door nails." He told me his brother Michael was on vacation and one of their other funeral directors wasn't going to be able to get there until right before the visitation.

"I need help moving Mr. Overton down to the viewing room," he said.

"Sure," I said, even if I wasn't so sure.

I had been in the funeral home before when bodies were already in the viewing room and situated in their caskets. Nowhere else, though. I wondered just for a second if Todd would mind if I called Wheat to see if she also wanted to help — ha, ha.

He led me up to the second floor where there are a couple of offices, a kitchen and the prep room, which is through a door off the kitchen. I don't think I could eat lunch up there. Sorry, spirits, that's just me.

"There are three bodies in here, including Mr. Overton," Todd said. "Are you sure you're okay with this? If your Dad's home,

I could call him. I know he has helped with removing bodies as a responding officer."

"I'm good," I said.

I took a deep breath and followed Todd through the kitchen and into the prep room. I took a quick look around and saw two people under sheets on tables with only their heads and toes showing. One was a gray-haired woman and one was a younger man.

"The lady there, Mrs. Johnson, pretty much died of old age — lived a wonderful life," Todd said. "And the big guy, Mr. Masters, died of a massive heart attack, leaving behind a wife and a couple kids. A real tragedy for everyone involved."

They both looked peaceful to me but as white as the sheets that covered them up to their necks. I had a hard time taking my eyes off them. I felt a certain responsibility to acknowledge that their lives had had meaning and they weren't just dead bodies. I'm thinking that's what I was thinking anyway.

Mr. Overton was over in the corner on a gurney, already dressed in a black suit with a reddish tie. He was a little man with a grey crewcut and a neatly trimmed mustache. An oak casket on a stand with wheels was beside him "Oh, wow," I said to Todd. "When you said we were going to move him, I was thinking we were going to have to carry him all the way down into the viewing room."

He laughed.

"Not the way we usually do it. You grab him by the feet and I'll take his shoulders and we'll put him in the casket. Mr. Overton was a steel worker over in Gary for most of his life — hard and sometimes dangerous work. I know his daughter, Sue. She said he was always active and never had an ounce of fat on him. She said he never weighed more than 150 pounds and after he battled some health problems, I weighed him at 118 pounds yesterday. That's why I figured you could help me."

I didn't feel it was the appropriate time to mention that Mr. Overton would have been in my wrestling weight class.

I hesitated just for a moment and then grabbed him by the ankles and we lifted him into the open casket. It wasn't as creepy as I thought it would be. Then I helped Todd wheel the casket to the little elevator lift at the far end of the prep room. I didn't even know it existed until then.

It is an open shaft with a carpeted lift floor that works with an electric pulley. Todd told me it went all the way down into the basement where extra caskets and other supplies are stored.

We rode it to the first floor, where the lift is hidden behind a couple of white double doors. We then wheeled the gurney and the casket with Mr. Overton in it into the viewing room. Todd worked a little on Mr. Overton's makeup and placed a picture of his family and a little Bible in the casket beside him. He then set a White Sox cap up by his head.

"A great fan, his daughter said," Todd added as I watched from a few feet back. "And he hated the Cubs — but we'll overlook that."

Being a Cub fan, I didn't like hearing that so much. But the other stuff and the fact that he was a baseball fan made me feel a certain connection with Mr. Overton. He wasn't just a body anymore to me. He was somebody's father, probably a grandfather, too, a hard worker and a sports fan. I think I would have probably liked him.

After Todd straightened Mr. Overton's tie, he said, "Billy Ray, I usually say a little prayer after I have people situated. It's just something I do. There will be enough prayers said over him later today at the visitation and then at his funeral tomorrow. But since I prepared him for his final destination, I feel like I've had a chance to glimpse a little bit of his soul as it departs. You don't have to, but I'm inviting you to join me if you would like."

I did. And Todd said a nice prayer about what a decent man that Mr. Overton had been. At the end, he brought a little humor into it by saying, "And help those Chicago teams with some winning, Mr. Overton, including the Cubs."

I had to work hard not to start misting up. I've said my prayers at night since I was a little kid and I bow my head and listen as intently as I can as our minister prays during Sunday service. Yet this was the first time a prayer really felt like it hit home for me.

As I got ready to leave, Todd handed me two $20 bills.

"That's way too much," I said.

"I didn't pay you for the last time you shoveled the walk and the way the forecast looks, I might need you in the next couple of days. And if we get the warm spell they're predicting, I wouldn't mind if you shoveled around our basketball goal out back. I need some exercise and a chance to put my little brother in his place."

I said I could do that and started thinking about his brother Michael being called little at 6-foot-4. I also thought that the money would come in handy for a corsage for Laurie. Mom told me we needed to get her one. But mostly, I thought of Mr. Overton and his life.

When I got home, I knew Wheat was going to ask me if I saw any bodies. And she did before I got my boots off. I told her I saw three and let it go at that. She didn't look like she wanted to ask any more questions anyway. At some point, I figured I would ask Ric about his experience with going into a house where a person has died. I guess I no longer believe in ghosts. Maybe spirits, but not ghosts.

After dinner — vegetarian pizza — I thought about calling Laurie. In fact, I had thought about calling her all weekend. But I couldn't come up with what I would say. I sometimes watch those TV shows with teenagers always spewing out clever things on the phone. I didn't think I could do that. I was starting to think that having a crush on somebody is a lot easier than actually having some sort of relationship with them, no matter how insignificant it might be.

I prayed for Mr. Overton's soul that night and the other two people in the prep room although I couldn't remember their names. I also prayed for my biological dad's soul. I hadn't thought of him in a while and I felt a little guilty. His name was John and he sold farm equipment. He was sick during a lot of the time I knew him. He had been a good dad, though, and never complained about having to be in bed so much.

I just wish he could have been well enough to play some pitch-and-catch with me or go fishing. I think my best memory of him was camping in our tent in the backyard before he got too sick and building almost a whole city with Lego. Mom said that he could build about anything before his illness.

I got to say goodbye to him at the hospital a few hours before he died. He told me to take care of mom. I'm glad I have Ric to help me with that now. I think my real dad — John — would be happy that my newer dad — Ric — is with Mom and me now.

I'm guessing this, but I bet they would have liked each other. And I don't think my first dad would mind me calling my second dad by Dad. It's been four years, after all. I think both of them can fit okay in my life — Ric in person and John in my memories.

CHAPTER 11

Most of Monday was mundane. I like how that sentence sounds. When I write stuff for English, I always like to use some alliteration. Maybe I use it too much. But Mrs. Murphy seems to like it.

Part of the reason things weren't that exciting was that Laurie wasn't in English class — her friend Debbie who sits a row behind me said she had a cold — and I got a B-minus on a history test. I guess I studied the wrong chapter. I had studied the one on Lewis and Clark, but I was supposed to know all about the Louisiana Purchase. I already knew something about that and so I didn't do too terrible. But a B-minus is still a B-minus.

If I hadn't named my frogs Notre and Dame, I figure that Lewis and Clark might be good names for them, although they don't get to do too much exploring around their aquariums. Someday, I wouldn't mind making a pond outside for them. But then they might head out for some long-range exploring like Lewis and Clark did.

Finding out Laurie was sick made me feel a little bad that I hadn't called her. I could have told her to get well. But then again, maybe I would have just ended up getting her off the couch when she wasn't in the mood to talk. Or maybe her dad would have answered the phone and told me to stay away from his daughter. Too many what-ifs there.

Practice was all about getting ready for Mishawaka on Tuesday. Coach Mathews went over our various match-ups and he acted like we could win the meet. He always acts like we can win every meet with a top opponent but this time I really think he believed it. Mishawaka is ranked 7th in the state so it would be very big if we could.

Wheat and I got home and had to really hustle to get ready for our ballroom dancing class. I let her go first in the shower since she said she wanted to wash her hair. I ended up having to eat a grilled cheese sandwich in the back of Dad's squad car on our way to the class.

I'm not telling Mom this but I am sort of liking the dancing this year. I never thought I would say that. I hate wearing the coat and tie that gets my neck all itchy. I hate all the little formalities that Mrs. Gray makes us go through, like getting punch for the girls midway through the lesson and bowing and curtseying like we're in one of those old British movies. But I do sort of like the dancing.

Wheat does, too. And Bobby Taylor really likes it because Wheat is in the class. I'm a lot better dancer than Bobby and if I say so myself, I'm probably a little better than Wheat. We don't say anything about that but I think she knows it. Hmmm, maybe I should say something.

Mrs. Gray sometimes even uses me to help demonstrate a dance. Hey, I do get $5 a session as a junior assistant instructor. She says I'm a fast learner. Her real assistant instructors are all older girls but they need some goof to serve as their partner when they demonstrate.

Jessica Lercher even gives me a little smile when I am the one to join her. I'm an inch or two taller than last year and so I can almost look her in the eye — or at least up her nose — and my guiding hand knows just where to go.

Every time I put it on the small of her back, she says, "Now keep your hands right where they are, pardner," like I'm thinking about having a shootout with her or something. She hasn't forgotten my little faux paus — I think that's French for being a dufus — but I'm glad she has a sense of humor.

We have the dance class in a big Masonic Hall with a giant dance floor and there are probably 120 of us from the eight high schools in South Bend and nearby Mishawaka. This was the fourth lesson of the year — no lesson last week, though, because Mrs. Gray was out of town — and we were going to work on the foxtrot.

About the time we were ready to start, who walked into the hall but Big Jim and Sally Guffie? I about had a panic attack. They hadn't said anything about it on our morning ride. In fact, I don't remember Sally saying anything to me the last three days of our rides to school. And I'm not sure they even knew that Wheat and I took lessons. I had to look at them a couple of times just to make sure it was them.

Big Jim looked like Shrek in a suit — only more pink than green — but Sally looked like somebody that could cause other girls to stare at her with envy and guys to …. well, stare like guys do. Seriously. She had on a pretty yellow dress and her hair up in a way that I guess still hid her horns. I'm not kidding, the first thing I thought about was Beauty and the Beast. Who would ever guess that they were brother and sister?

But the number one surprise of the night was that Sally didn't look like she felt totally in charge of the situation. In fact, I thought she looked a little bit nervous. Ha, ha, I thought. What comes around …

And just then, Mrs. Gray did the unthinkable.

"Oh, yes, our new students. Jessica, why don't you work with the young man and Billy Ray, would you please help our new young lady?"

Sally seemed relieved and actually smiled at me, but not enough to show her fangs.

"Well, Little Man, so you're going to show me the ropes?" she said as she walked up to me, her hand held out in an exaggerated way.

I guess her nervousness was suddenly over — or well-hidden.

I stood my ground.

"You can call me Billy Ray or Spanky or even Sir William of South Bend if you want, but don't call me Little Man anymore. If you do, you can go over there and stand by the punch bowl until some guy nerdier than me comes over and asks you to dance," I said.

Sally looked at me with amusement.

"Well then, Sir William it is," she said.

And with that, I led her through a foxtrot. We were actually pretty good together. I mean we weren't going to get 10's on "Dancing with the Stars," but we at least might have looked like we had a clue. She had a nice glide to her. Unlike a lot of girls who are a little bigger than me, Sally didn't make me fight her for the lead. That surprised me, too.

After the dance, Mrs. Gray went over the steps of the waltz that we had worked on two weeks ago. Usually, I would dance with the girl who ended up on my left but Sally held onto my hand. So we danced together again.

"You're really good, Sir William," she said. "Who would have guessed?"

"You're not so bad yourself," I replied. "And you're here because ...?"

"My brother thought it might be good for his balance in sports and since I'm probably going to the winter formal with one of my suitors, I thought I might as well brush up on my dancing, too. I won't tell any of them, though, that you've been teaching me some new moves."

I admitted to myself that might not go over so well with Kelly Carson or anybody else of his ilk — another of my new words and maybe the smallest. Did I tell you yet that one of my favorite books is the Thesaurus? Yep, I'm a word weenie. And how do you like that alliteration?

We went to some more incredible instruction — ha, ha, — and Sally and I ended up with other partners. When we broke for punch, I noticed that five or six guys were trying to situate themselves in line so they could pair up with Sally. I thought they might survive if they stayed in a pack.

Wheat and I usually try to stay as far away from each other as possible so we don't end up as dancing partners. It's funny that we can get in all sorts of entanglements on the wrestling mat but we don't want anything to do with each other when it comes to dancing.

But she wandered over to me after — who else — Bobby Taylor had gotten her punch.

"You and your Carpool Love looked pretty good out there," she said.

I just shook my head. I couldn't say much. I'm always teasing her about how Bobby is making sure he can get at least one dance with her. He has to work at it because she is pretty popular with the guys, too.

Then Wheat grimaced.

"Get away from me if you're going to eat those cookies," she added.

Yeah, I was helping myself to the cookies by the punch. Like Wheat, I had to pass on the cookies when I was wrestling 113 behind her. So I moved away but not before I opened my mouth so Wheat could see the chunks of a chocolate chip cookie in my mouth.

Just as well that Mrs. Gray didn't see me do that. She may have called a f-f-f-f-fortnight of fouls on me — ha, ha, ha.

During the rest of the lesson, I tried to dance with the girls who are shy or who aren't very coordinated. That's what Dad said I should do and I think it's a good idea, too. He said that those are the girls who often work hard, grow up and really make something of themselves when they blossom later. But I still kept an eye on Sally just to see how she was doing. Her yellow dress made it easy to keep her in sight.

As my mom would say, she was the Belle of the Ball, even if it was her first lesson.

We have a handful of Kelly Carson-type guys in our class and they all were a little agog about Sally. But on the last dance — girls' choice — she actually trotted up to me and grabbed my hand. Yikes!

Mrs. Gray was letting all of us do our own version of fast dancing to a cool country song, "She was a Heartthrob on the Dance Floor" by Jon Pardi. At one point, Sally did a circle dance around me like she was rounding me up like livestock. It was pretty great. Mrs. Gray even cracked a smile, probably for the first time in a fortnight. Love that word, too, even thought I would never use it in everyday conversation.

I was thinking this was a pretty cool night. When the dance was over, Sally walked over to her brother to leave.

She then looked over her shoulder and called back to me, "Thanks for being my partner, Little Man."

Pop!

CHAPTER 12

Bobby's dad took us home and we scurried into the house. It was already 8:30 and both Wheat and I had some homework still to do. We also had our big dual meet the next evening against Mishawaka and we like to be in bed by 9:30, especially before meet nights.

We both have desks in our room but to make them fit, they have to be pushed up against each other. So we face each other when we both sit there, although I have a big ceramic frog on the back of my desk and she has a couple of her wrestling trophies on hers. Her trophies are bigger than my frog, of course. We end up having to peek around them if we want to ask each other a question.

Since we have the same sophomore courses — and are in the same algebra class — we do help each other out. That's mostly good but there are a few times when I wouldn't mind having a little private time with my own thoughts. Don't get me wrong. Wheat is great to have around and talk to, but sometimes a girl is still a girl.

I didn't really feel like talking about Sally but I knew Wheat would.

And so as soon as I opened my algebra book, she said, "I think you might want to watch your step, bro. I just don't see Sally Guffie being that nice to you without some kind of ulterior motive. I don't know if it has something to do with Kelly Carson or Laurie Middlebrook or what but I would watch her if I were you."

"Oh, I will," I said and I knew she could be right.

The evening had been exciting but a little uncomfortable, too. Although I enjoyed most of my time with Sally, I had enough beauty on my mind with Laurie.

"I had one dance with Big Jim," she continued. "What a klutz. He supposedly wants to work on his footwork. His dad apparently convinced him that it might help him on the offensive line if he can get a scholarship for football at a small college. But the interesting thing is what he said about Sally."

I was all ears. I waited. She didn't say anything. I waited some more. Wheat smiled but still didn't say anything.

"Okay, okay," I said. "Tell me."

She paused another couple of seconds before spilling the beans.

"Big Jim says that their grandmother really gave it to Sally at Sunday dinner. Told her she had become a spoiled brat — a nasty nellie, whatever that means. Her grandma went on to say that just because she had turned out really pretty that she didn't have to act like a prima donna.

"According to Big Jim," Wheat continued, "Sally has always adored her grandma and so the lecture really hit her hard. She started crying right at the table and Big Jim couldn't remember the last time he saw her shed any tears. Her mom tried to come to her rescue but Granny Goodwrench told her to butt out. Sally finally admitted that maybe she could be a little nicer. Big Jim says that's why they enrolled in the dancing so Sally could work on her manners."

"It was their grandma's suggestion — or maybe command — and she's paying for the lessons. She apparently is an old friend of Mrs. Gray's and that's how they got in after the lessons had already started. Big Jim had to go to even up the boy-girl count just like us. One thing is certain: Their grandma apparently is somebody who says it like it is."

"Geez," I said. "Sally told me they were there to work on Jim's footwork."

"Well, that wouldn't be a bad idea, either," Wheat added. "My feet could tell you that. But the main reason is that Sally needs to be more of a young lady, according to her grandma."

We weren't getting much algebra done. So I asked her a question.

"You and Big Jim seemed to hit it off pretty good."

"We were okay with each other," was all that Wheat said in return.

"Sooo....?"

"Well, it you want to know the truth, he hinted at going to the winter formal with me but I told him that he and I would both probably be in the championship round of the conference meet Saturday evening and that would interfere with it. That seemed to do the trick. Just as well. He's always been an okay guy but not my type although he did look half way decent dressed up."

"You mean Shrek?" I almost shouted.

"He's not that bad. You know he's always been very protective of me at wrestling. And to be honest, the starting time of the 113-pound title match would make it a lot easier for me to get to the formal but him at heavyweight would probably make us pretty late. Anyway, it's not worth even thinking about."

I tried to digest all that she had said. I never had given it any thought when Laurie had asked me to the winter formal that I might be tied up with the conference meet. But I wasn't planning on qualifying for the championship round — too many good 120-pounders in the conference. I was going to be happy not to be pinned in the first round.

"No way Big Jim is getting to the championship round," I eventually said. "Let him think so but he won't. He's barely a .500 wrestler. You could probably get to most of the winter formal even if you win and Coach lets you head out."

"I don't need to go to any dance," she said.

"But it's nice you sort of got asked, right?"

"Hey, if you want to count that, then I've been asked four times. Your buddy Bobby asked me at dance lessons. Thirsty asked me at practice Friday while I had him in a half-nelson and that Paul guy in my biology class asked. He's a little creepy but he's one smart dude and is more than happy to help me understand some of that crazy animal anatomy."

I was stunned. She had never mentioned any of this to me.

"And you didn't tell me all of that?" I asked.

"You didn't tell me about Laurie Middlebrook, either," Wheat replied. "And I said no to all of them so there's not really any news here. I plan on being in the conference championship and rooting our team on to victory after that."

She was right. I hadn't told her about Laurie. But I shouldn't have been surprised that she has been asked multiple times. I guess I don't always realize — her being my sister and all — that Wheat is really a pretty girl besides being smart and somewhat sweet in her own way.

I didn't want to think of this too much, though, because I like her as my roommate and close confidante. And I didn't want a mental picture of her being slobbered over by a bunch of guys who have fewer social skills than I do —which, as you have probably figured out by now, isn't a whole lot.

I wondered if I ought to mention to Mom about Wheat's proposals. I know Wheat wouldn't say anything and Mom is always worried that Wheat is a little too tomboyish. Of course, I bet Ric probably thinks that I'm a little on the sissyish side. I would agree with him. I do lean a little bit that way but the wrestling seems to help me hide some of my timid tendencies — yeah, I can even use alliteration when I'm weighing my weaknesses.

If I hadn't been wrestling, no way I would probably stand up to — or fall into — Kelly or chase after the One-Booted Man.

Ha, ha. I came up with that one after remembering "The Fugitive" movie with Harrison Ford chasing after a One-Armed Man. Dad thought the name was pretty funny, too. It even made him think about watching that movie again.

That's one of the reasons I love that Mom and I melded into a family with Wheat and Dad. I would probably be a bit of a lost soul without them. I don't tell Wheat this but she has pulled out a part of my personality that may never have come to the surface if she hadn't been around. And I sure have met a lot of interesting people because of her and Ric — I mean Dad.

I think I wouldn't even have the nerve to speak to a girl like Laurie Middlebrook if it weren't for Wheat. To tell you the truth, I'm still pretty afraid of girls. But not as much as I used to be. It's funny that a girl who beats me up makes me more confident around her type — if Wheat actually has a type. Enough of that for now, okay?

Before we turned off the light after getting in bed, I did say, "Wheat, you may be the only person in history who has been asked out to the same dance by a guy who doesn't even weigh 100 pounds and one who probably goes about 260."

"Why don't you call the Guinness Book of World Records, Spank?" she asked with a sarcastic tone. "I'm sure you and Laurie Middlebrook going to the winter formal together might qualify for some category, too. And who knows, maybe you and her could also be a new telling of an old story — Beauty and the Little Beasty."

I figured I better back off or it might get nasty.

"Night, Wheat," I said.

"Night, Little Beasty," she replied as I frowned to myself about another nickname. "And if you tell Mom and Dad that I was asked to the formal by those guys, I'll stuff you in your pillow case."

I stayed quiet. She probably could do it.

CHAPTER 13

The next morning, we got up and ran even though we had a meet that night. I just can't talk Wheat out of it. I sometimes wonder if she is a masochist — or maybe just the opposite since it seems sort of sadistic that she always seems to take delight in making me do it too. I went along without complaining, though.

We were pretty quiet. Dad must not have even felt like singing. I think he hurt his leg the other morning more than he has let on. I asked him if there were any leads on the One-Booted Man and his accomplice. He said no but that car break-ins around town had spiked in the last couple of months. Those guys were prime suspects.

When we got home, we weighed ourselves. Wheat was at 112 and I tipped the scales at a whopping 115 pounds while stripped down to my underwear. Heaviest I've ever been. I almost felt fat — ha, ha.

"I'm eating some pancakes if Mom will make Lake and me some," I announced. "And I'm going to drench them in syrup."

"Rub it in," Wheat said. "I thought I was happy for you getting the varsity spot at 120, but now I'm not so sure."

Wheat loves pancakes and syrup but only allows herself to have them about four times a year, usually right after wrestling season. Lake loves them, too, and since he doesn't like milk much or even cereal— weird kid — Mom makes them a lot for him and Rrrrr — Dad.

She is very creative in the shapes she makes out of the pancake mix. She can come up with all kinds of animals and other stuff. As a kindergarten teacher, you probably need to be pretty good at it and like all that crazy art that little kids come up with. I guess you need to like little kids, too. Mom does.

So after I told her I wanted pancakes, she said she would make me up a special design.

Lake got a couple of bunnies, equipped with ears and bushy tails. I got what looked like a couple of cut-out dolls holding hands.

Before I could say anything, Lake looked over at the creation on my plate and said, "That?"

"Yeah, that," Wheat chimed in as she sipped her six ounces of skim milk and peeled a tangerine across the table from me.

"That's Billy Ray and Laurie dancing at the winter formal," Mom proudly said.

To be honest, it was a pretty darn good creation but the subject almost made me lose my appetite. This could be something that Wheat could tease me about endlessly.

"Want that," Lake announced.

I would have traded him, too, but he had one of his bunnies almost devoured and even taking his age into account, he may be the messiest eater of all time. His plate looked like a bunch of Play-Doh globs with orange juice poured around it.

"I'll make you cute little Billy Ray and Laurie dancers tomorrow," Mom said to him.

"Mom!" I cried.

"Mom!" Lake mimicked.

Dad then walked into the kitchen wearing his police uniform. I always look on in wonder when I see him decked out in his working blue. He looks like the perfect cop. He looks like the guy you would want busting down your front door when somebody evil has already busted down your back door. He is a street sergeant although his bosses really would like him to transfer over to the detective bureau.

"Hey, I see that Spank has joined the pancake posse today," he said. "What's the shape?"

Before I could say anything, Wheat said, "That's him and Laurie dancing at the winter formal. She looks so good that I'm sure Spank can't wait to just eat her up. Yum, yum."

Ric and Mom laughed and Lake smiled widely even though he didn't have any idea what we were talking about.

Wheat wasn't done, though.

"Or maybe it's Sally Guffie. You should have seen Spank and her on the dance floor last night."

That did it!

"Well, you should have seen Wheat and her beaus," I said. "How many guys have asked you to the winter formal now, Wheat? Wasn't the count up to four as of last night?"

"Is that true, Tanda?" Mom said.

"Ta-Da?" Lake asked as if he had never heard his sister called by her real name.

"Yeah, that's Miss Popularity across from the table from you, Lake," I said and proceeded to eat my pancakes, trying not to imagine whether the girl was Laurie or Sally.

Wheat had stormed off at that point. I wasn't going to get near her. But I didn't feel bad. She had started the teasing. And what did she say would happen to me — that she would stuff me in my pillow case? Hey, that doesn't sound as bad as some of the holds she puts me in at wrestling practice.

"Is that true about the boys asking her," Mom started. And then she quickly added, "Well, of course it is."

"Would any of these potential beaus have a fighting chance with her," Dad chimed in.

"Only if Big Jim could figure out a way to get her in a bear hug," I said. "She's not going with any of them, though. The formal would interfere with the conference championship matches on Saturday night."

"Well, what about you, Spank?" Dad asked. "Aren't you still going to be the 120-pounder then?"

"Yeah, but no way 1 make it to the title match," I said. "Don't get me wrong. I'm doing a little better and will be trying my best. But a week ago, I was still a junior varsity wrestler at a lower weight."

I thought it might be wise to keep it to myself that I might want to go to the winter formal with Laurie Middlebrook more than being a conference champion. At least that was what I was thinking as I politely took a bite out of Laurie's — I mean the girl's — side of my pancake.

"What a busy Saturday," Mom said. "I do wish that Tanda could go to the dance. I do like that some boys seem to see her as more than a tomboy in wrestling togs. Do you think she likes boys, Spank? Do you?"

"Sure," I said. "Especially after she beats them up."

Dad laughed. Mom just shook her head. Lake said Ta-Da again. He seemed to like that name. Actually, I sort of liked it, too. There certainly are enough ta-da's when Wheat wrestles.

About that time, I heard the front door slam. Uh-oh. When I went up to the upstairs bathroom, I found a note by the sink.

"Dear Jerk," it started. "I'm jogging to school instead of pushing you out our window. Maybe you can make out with Sally in the backseat in my absence. P.S. I used your toothbrush to comb my hair."

Well, at least we were communicating. We live about three miles from the high school and so it wasn't any big deal for Wheat to run it, especially when she had some anger to work out of her system. But adding on to the four miles we already had covered before breakfast, that would give her seven miles on the day of a very big meet. Oh well, I thought, not my worry.

Big Jim seemed plenty worried, though, when he pulled up in front of our house.

"Where's Wheat?" he asked when I slid into the backseat. "She's not sick, is she? We need her if we have any chance to beat Mishawaka tonight."

"She's fine," I said. "In fact, she's fired up for a fight. She just decided to run to school. Making sure her weight is good for tonight."

I noticed Sally wasn't saying anything up in the front seat beside her brother. She had one of her textbooks out in her lap while Big Jim and I talked about how he thought the dancing from the previous night might really be good for his football and wrestling.

But when he pulled out in the parking lot and got out, Sally grabbed me gently by my coat and asked me to walk her into school. Her brother looked back at us and shook his head.

"You poor pooch, Spank," he said. Then he added, "Play nice, Sis."

"He's a bozo," Sally said as we walked slowly toward the school while I looked around for any signs of Laurie — or Kelly Carson. "But he's passable for an older brother, I suppose. I'm trying to see that in him a little more. We used to be closer when we were kids. I wouldn't mind trying to have a similar relationship that you have with your sister."

"Oh, ours isn't always fun and games, " I said.

"Probably none are. Just wanted to tell you that I appreciated your help last night at dance class. I enjoyed it and you are a good dancer. I'm trying to be a little nicer to people although I still couldn't keep myself from calling you 'Little Man' at the end. Being constantly nice is a little harder to do than I thought it would be."

I told her no big deal. I didn't tell her that I knew her grandma had come down hard on her. I tried not to think that she might be worrying about her inheritance or something. I hoped she wasn't just putting on an act.

"I might see you tonight at the meet," she added. "I haven't seen the Big Bro wrestle yet this year and so I figure it's time to make my one appearance at the House of Smells."

"House of Smells?"

"Come on, Sir William, you know how bad a wrestling room can stink."

I nodded. I wasn't going to argue with her, especially when her own brother — the smelliest of them all — was on the premises. Body odor and teen-age hormones revved up for combat are a pretty deadly mix. I guess I've gotten used to it over the last couple of years, though. It even makes me feel at home in some ways. I'm not going to try to explain that to you — or me.

"By the way," Sally said. "What's worse in your opinion? Being called 'poor pooch' by my brother or 'little man' by me?"

"Depends on the situation," I replied. "But someday, I'm hoping they call me rich man."

She smiled — gosh she was pretty when she smiled.

As I held the door open for her to go into school, she smiled again and said, "Didn't you think that your sister and my brother looked a little like Beauty and the Beast last night?"

"No, doubt about it," I replied, not telling her that I had been called the Little Beasty myself the previous night.

Sally then walked down the hallway. As always, a lot of heads turned in her direction and I thought this time that she still looked a little like Katy Perry as she strutted toward her locker. I tried to imagine her as suddenly transforming into a Snow White while I looked on as one of her "little men" — Dopey probably being the best fit.

As I would have predicted, Wheat ignored me in algebra class. Then Kelly Carson came out of Mrs. Riley's classroom between classes as I was passing and actually gave me a brief nod.

"What's his story?" Bobby Taylor asked.

"Not sure, but I'm not going over to give him a fist bump and find out."

In English class right before the bell, Laurie, still with a red nose from her cold, touched my arm and asked if it would be okay if we just met at the high school gym for the winter formal. She said her dad was having a hard time with her going out at all and thought I might not be the perfect person to take her. She laughed when she told me that but I think she was a little bothered that he had said that. Maybe she was wondering a little, too.

"What's that all about?" I had to ask.

"Well, he never really approved of me seeing Kelly Carson. He thought he was a little on the rough side although he was always pretty nice to me. And then he shows up right after you knocked down Kelly. I told him that you did it in the name of chivalry but he's just a little concerned."

"I thought he had been a wrestler," I said.

"Maybe, maybe not," Laura said. "With Dad, you're never quite sure. He doesn't seem like the wrestling type to me. Maybe he thinks a sport looks good on his resume. He's a bit of a hypochondriac, according to mom. And she kids that the only exercise he gets now is jumping to conclusions."

I nodded but I didn't get it. Then when I walked her down the hall, still getting some good looks, it suddenly hit me. Jumping — jumping to conclusions. I laughed.

"What's that?" Laurie said, looking a little like I might be laughing at her for some reason.

"Delayed reaction on your mom's joke," I said.

"Glad you got it, Spank," she said, stopping at her biology classroom. "Now get, get," she said with a smile.

After our conversation, I got this tingling feeling that took a while to go away. Like I've said, deep down, I'm still a bit of a wuss. I know it, Wheat knows it and Dad knows it. But the mayor of South Bend thinks I'm some kind of tough guy. And maybe his daughter thinks so a little, too. This might sound surprising, but I kind of felt good about that. I know this reputation thing isn't going to last but I thought I might enjoy being a bad boy for a little while longer.

I sure wasn't going to tell her that it was just a clumsy fall into Kelly that put him on the ground. If some people wanted to think I was like the Karate Kid or something, I wasn't doing to disagree.

I noticed that Laurie hadn't said anything about the meet. She probably didn't even know we were wrestling against Mishawaka.

CHAPTER 14

When I saw Wheat after school, she seemed okay with me. In fact, it was as if nothing had happened between us in the morning. Hmmmm… that was a little strange.

We don't have practice on days of the meets and so we both headed upstairs after Big Jim drove us home from school. Sally had apparently gotten another ride home. We hit the homework hard. Mom said that Todd Dixon had called and had wondered if I could shovel their walks before tomorrow morning. We'd gotten what looked like another two inches while we were in school.

After I solved a few algebra problems and did a biology worksheet, I started getting ready to shovel. I like getting that call. If the snow isn't too heavy, I can finish it in about a half hour and get $20 for it — vastly overpaid on those kinds of days. They have a guy with a plow on his truck who comes through for the parking lot at about 5 in the morning after it snows. It wakes me up sometimes but I don't mind. It's usually the sound of money for me, too.

"I'll help," Wheat said. "You need to conserve your strength for the meet tonight."

"Well, so do you," I said.

"Not as much as you. If you had looked at the results in the paper last Friday, you would have seen that Donnie Thompson went up to 120 for Mishawaka. He got third in the state last year at 113. And, as you probably remember, he beat me last month in the Hobart Invitational, 5-4. You got him tonight. I got some kid named Drinkman who had been junior varsity until Thompson decided to go up a weight."

"Great," I said. "Why did you wait to tell me this until now?"

"I didn't want you skipping town."

"I ought to let Tommy the Torso move up from behind you and take on this guy. I don't want to be dismembered before the big dance."

"Yeah, well I don't want to be surrounded by a couple of inept wrestlers for the varsity. Thirsty also has that kid who qualified for the state at 106 last year and I don't see him lasting more than a minute. And The Torso? His back spends as much time on the mat as our team logo. You'll do fine. Thompson may underestimate you."

"Underestimation just may be my secret weapon," I said.

We quit talking as I went into the funeral home's garage and got the shovels. I took my time and let Wheat do a lot of the work. She was right. I needed to conserve my strength.

As we were finishing up, our shared cell phone rang in Wheat's coat pocket. I don't think I had heard it ring in about a month. Like I have said, it's usually just for emergencies and I was surprised that Wheat even had it on her.

She seemed eager to answer it, though.

"Hello … " she said. "Oh, yeah… well, that's nice of you… sure… see you."

Then she handed it to me with an evil grin.

"Who?" I mouthed.

"Your dance partner," she said almost too loud.

I was half-dreading, half-wanting to hear Sally Guffie's voice but it was Laurie.

"Hi, Spank," she said. "I was very thoughtless today. I forgot that you had a wrestling meet tonight and I wanted to wish you good luck. If I didn't have my little brother's piano recital tonight, I might have come."

"Well, thanks, Laurie," I said. "I might need that good luck just to survive tonight. This would have probably been a good night for your dad to come and see me because he would see I'm not very tough at all — not against the guy I'm facing."

"Is he a real big guy or something?"

"No, he might be a couple of pounds heavier than me but we always wrestle people about the same size as us."

"Well then, I'm betting you will beat him."

I didn't have anything to add.

"Where are you and Tanda right now?" Laurie asked to break the silence.

"Clearing a path to the funeral home," he said.

"Funny, Spank," she said, apparently thinking I was making a joke about my destination after my match. "You are going to do good. Think positive."

We bid our good-byes and I joined Wheat in front at the curb. She was staring at the window of the funeral home on our house's side.

"Do you think somebody's in there?" she asked.

"Probably a body. I suspect there's going to be a funeral tomorrow morning if they want the walks cleared off today."

She shuddered. I knew that was creepy for her. As tough and brave as Wheat is on the wrestling mat, that doesn't mean that some stuff can't scare her. I'm not going to make fun of her. Otherwise, she would probably tease me about my fear of flocks of Canada geese — and nasty chickens, especially roosters. Any kind of birds, really, but geese and chickens in particular. But that's a story for some other time.

Just about the time we finished, an old clunker of a car eased down our street and slowed even more when it got close to us.

The driver, a hairy-looking guy with a stocking hat yelled out, "Hey, you little…" — I'm not going to tell you what he called us.

Then he sped off.

"What was that all about?" Wheat shouted.

"I don't know," I said softly, "but that voice sounded a lot like the guy we chased on Saturday. The One-Booted Man."

———————

Before a dual meet, everyone has their own little routine. We get weighed to make sure we are eligible for our respective weight classes and then we can have our snacks. I like a little honey right out of the jar and Wheat drinks a Diet coke for the caffeine.

We go through our warm-up moves and work up a bit of a sweat and then head into the locker room where Coach Mathews gives us a little pep talk. Although nobody can help you when you're out on the mat, we still view wrestling as a team sport. Coach Mathews says that we can feed off each other's good performances.

This time, he mentioned that Clay hadn't beaten Mishawaka in a dual meet in 15 years — when he was a junior and wrestling for Clay. I didn't feel it was the appropriate time to ask what happened his senior year.

"I really think this is the night we do it," he said, a little emotion creeping into his voice. "If we truly believe we can beat them tonight, it can happen. But it will take every one of you doing your best."

Then Big Jim and Dion Borden, the two senior captains, said a few words with Dion using some X-rated sentences. I don't think he learned those bad words from his dad since he's a preacher. Dion could probably give a good sermon, too, because we all were yelling and jumping up and down and Wheat and I don't even like cussing.

The junior varsity meet had just ended and so Coach Mathews said to line up. We were pretty psyched after Dion's speech and we burst into the gym with Thirsty, our smallest wrestler, leading the way followed closely by Wheat and me and with Big Jim bringing up the rear of our 14-person line.

We circled the mat on the run while our school song played on the sound system. It can give me goose pimples — I admit it, I can be a little rah rah. I took a look into the stands and saw my parents and Lake. I also spied Sally Guffie in her cheerleader uniform and sitting with her parents a few rows down. And in the corner of the gym and down the hall a little, I caught a glimpse of what looked like Kelly Carson in his letterman's jacket.

Yikes! Didn't I have enough worries about Donnie Thompson during the meet without having to think about what Kelly Carson might do to me afterwards? Maybe he had heard that Sally and I were dancing together the night before. I just hoped that Billy Brayton's promise to protect me was still on.

I wanted to tell Wheat but we were already lining up for our handshakes with Mishawaka. We walked across the mat and I noticed that Donnie Thompson didn't even look at me when he barely shook my hand, giving about all his attention to Wheat as she passed him by on his left.

Wrestling probably seems like a pretty simple sport to a lot of people. You get on top of a person and hold him down longer than he can do the same to you. I guess that's the basics but there's a lot of intricate moves you can use to get an advantage. Yeah, it's important to be strong and tough, but being perceptive and unpredictable are pretty good traits to have, too.

Points? I won't bore you with everything but you get one for an escape (breaking out of an opponent's hold) and two points for both a takedown (taking an opponent to the mat and gaining control) and a reversal (regaining control). You earn a pin when you have both of the other guy's shoulders on the mat. Got it? Explain it to my mom if you do.

After the introductions, I always head to the bench with my teammates. Wheat, the second one up, usually goes into the auxiliary gym through some double doors to do a few quick pushups and some sort of breathing exercises she learned from Uncle Mason. Here lately, I guess she has been applying her Midnight Breeze, too.

Just before her match, Wheat likes to burst out of the doors like a girl on fire. We saw the actor Matthew Modine do that in the wrestling and coming-of-age movie "Vision Quest," and she really liked it. Another one of Dad's favorites, of course.

But she didn't get much time because Thirsty got literally picked up and thrown down at the start of his match. After 14 seconds, the ref slammed his hand on the mat signifying a pin for the little Mishawaka wrestler with a name that would never fit on the back of his uniform even if he was the size of Big Jim. Vandergriffronald. Curtis Vandergriffronald. That's some mouthful. He looked even smaller than Thirsty but he wore an "I mean business" look on his face.

Fourteen seconds. That was even Thirsty's record — if you can have records for incompetence. A dozen of his 16 matches have ended in him getting pinned. His only victory was a kid who looked like he was in sixth grade. Well, at least he is out there giving it a try, I guess.

Our student manager, Maddie Hamilton, was hurrying off to get Wheat just as she came through the double doors. She almost knocked poor Maddie down with her hustle and bustle into the gym. Then she did something I have never see her do before. She actually took her eye off her opponent and scanned the gym, located Kelly who had taken a seat at the far end of the bleachers and gave him just the smallest of waves.

I might as well had been knocked over by a tidal wave. Kelly Carson? And never in my life had I ever seen her not try to win a stare-down with her opponent from the moment she comes into the gym.

I guess it didn't matter. She scored a takedown on the Drinkman kid and then almost pinned him before the first two-minute period was over. She was ahead 5-0 going into the second period and then ended it with a quick rollover move.

I usually do a little jump roping when I am next up but I was so mesmerized with whatever Wheat and Kelly had between them that I just stared in wonder — looking from Kelly to Wheat on the mat and then back again.

Our team, meanwhile, was feeling pretty confident. After two matches, we were tied with the mighty Mishawaka and now it was my turn to build on the momentum that Wheat had given us. I think my emotions were so high that I immediately scored a takedown on Donnie Thompson before he knew what was happening. He may have taken me for granted. Maybe Wheat was right.

And then again, maybe she wasn't. Thompson quickly reversed me and I realized I was going to have to hang on for dear life. In the second period, I did score on an escape but it was 7-3 heading into the third and final period.

I spent most of it on my back and the last minute with Thompson trying to pin both my shoulders flat onto the mat. In a situation like that, I try to think of beautiful females. I don't know why. It must get my adrenaline pumping. I thought of the actress Elle Fanning, I thought of Millie Bobby Brown of "Stranger Things," I thought of Laurie Middlebrook, I thought of Sally Guffie, I even thought of Mrs. Riley, imagining her when she was the Miss

Delaware second runner-up. Somehow I managed to keep my right shoulder an inch or so from the mat.

I know it frustrated Thompson even if he won, 12-3. That meant that Mishawaka only got three points for the team standings instead of the six if he had pinned me. I know my team was happier with that outcome than our opponents were.

While I recovered on the bench and after I got high fives from everybody and a slap on the butt from Wheat, I scanned the crowd again. My parents looked happy, Sally gave me sort of a "What's up?" sign with her outstretched hands — I couldn't tell if that was a compliment or criticism — and Kelly Carson was nowhere to be found.

Dion Borden put us back in the lead with a third-period pin and my whole focus was on my teammates who all did really well. When Big Jim held on to in the heavyweight match, 8-7, we had won the meet, 36-34.

A lot of our fans — maybe about 80 — charged onto the mat. A couple of our bigger teammates tried to lift Big Jim onto their shoulders but soon gave up on the idea. But then Big Jim lifted Wheat up in the air like she was Tinkerbell. His sister had come out of the stands and when she saw her brother's celebration, she headed toward me. I was halfway expecting one of her taunting kisses but instead she picked me up in a bear hug like I was a sack of potatoes. In a million years, I would have never guessed that that was going to happen.

Sally is maybe two inches taller than me and probably outweighs me by 20 pounds or so. I just never thought of her as somebody who would bother lifting anything heavier than her purse.

When she set me down, she said, "My dad said that if that meanie Mishawaka man (can alliteration be contagious?) had pinned you, you guys wouldn't have won the meet, Sir William. He also said just watching you almost gave him a hernia. So, I guess it was a nice loss."

All I could say was, "I didn't know you were so strong."

She then walked over to her brother and gave him a wind-up slap on the butt. Ouch! And then I was suddenly down on the mat as my own sister tackled me and a few of our teammates joined us in the pile. Even Maddie Hamilton, who is usually pretty shy, gave me a high five.

Coach Mathews had lost his voice from yelling so much during the match but he still was able to give a great victory speech back in the locker room. He was pretty emotional. For some reason, his raspy voice reminded me of the guy in the brown car and maybe the One-Booted Man but I soon forgot about it.

Although Wheat uses the girls' locker room down the hall to change, she is in the boys' locker room a good portion of the time for our meetings and other stuff. So is Maddie for that matter. I don't think anybody really cares. Like me, I think the guys don't even look at Wheat as a girl when she's wrestling. But I guess I'm finding out that Big Jim and Thirsty and maybe some of the others must think that she is at least winter formal-worthy when she's not in her uniform.

On the way home, we sat on both sides of Lake in his baby seat in the back of Dad's squad car. Both he and Mom were beaming and Lake kept saying, "Winnnnn!" and "Pinnnnn!" Like I already told you, he probably already knows as much about wrestling as Mom does.

He then added a "Ta-Da" and pointed at Wheat — or Tanda in this case.

"Well, Wheat," I said. "Maybe you have a new nickname."

I didn't tell her that Sally had started calling me Sir William. To be honest, I kind of liked it.

CHAPTER 15

It wasn't until we were upstairs and getting ready for bed before I asked Wheat about Kelly Carson. "What's the deal with him at the meet? It seems he was there to watch you — and that you knew he was going to be there."

"I could say none of your business, Spank, but since it's partly your fault, I'll tell you a story. When you were such a jerk at breakfast and I decided to jog to school, he drove by and picked me up in his Mustang. I wasn't sure I wanted to get in, but he made one of his buddies get in the backseat so I could ride shotgun. He then apologized for the night at Mug and Munchies. He seemed to mean it. Then he walked me into school and asked if it would be okay if he came to watch me wrestle. He said he would feel a lot better to see that he wasn't the only guy I could whip."

"Wow, you better watch Sally Guffie. She might think you're stealing her winter formal date."

"That came up and he said there was nothing to that. They've known each other forever. They've been at the same school since kindergarten and their parents play cards on a lot of the weekends. They've done stuff as families. He did call her the other night. I think he was maybe thinking about asking her to the formal but he never did. He just looks at her as a good friend. No sparks there, according to him. He's probably seen enough of her ugly side over the years. He worries that she intimidates boys a little too much for her own good. She may not even end up with a date to the formal."

Hmm, that was interesting, but I certainly could see that.

"So did Kelly ask you to the big dance?" I asked.

"None of your business, Big Mouth. As I said before, I plan on being wrestling for a conference championship Saturday night."

"What a crazy last couple of days," I said, thinking it was time to change the subject.

Wheat was looking out the window toward the funeral home.

"I hate to ask again, but do you really think there's a body over there right now?"

"Yeah, and its ghost is coming after you tonight."

Then I ran off and locked the bathroom door behind me. I might be as scared of an angry Wheat as she is of wandering ghosts. I took my time doing my bathrooming and finished by brushing my teeth. I then hid my toothbrush behind the Band-Aids in the closet in case Wheat wanted to mess with it again.

When I opened up the door, I could see Wheat on our cell phone in the room. When she saw me, she cut off her conversation with a quick "goodbye."

"Who were you talking to?" I asked, thinking I already knew.

"The Ghostbusters," she said. "I can sleep soundly now."

I wasn't sure I could. Life seemed a lot less complicated when I wasn't a wrestling star — ha, ha — and when the cool people in school were leaving Wheat and me alone.

I had a really weird dream that night. I won't go into all the details but I was wrestling Kelly Carson and I was ticked off because Wheat was coaching him and giving him instructions from the sidelines. When I finally won, I wouldn't shake either of their hands. Kelly was crying and Wheat was trying to soothe him. I felt like I had lost even though I had won.

The dream didn't seem to end. I started to leave the gym, not bothering to change out of my uniform, only to see that Laurie Middlebrook and Sally Guffie were getting ready to wrestle. Sally had on a cape and did some flying kick that sent Laurie into the bleachers. Laurie's dad — the mayor — then came onto the mat and

Sally put him in a headlock and he started yelling uncle. Then she pinned Big Jim, her brother. At that point, she looked at me and asked if I wanted to dance. She didn't call me Sir William. She called me Little Man.

I woke up then. Yuck. I was sweating like I really had wrestled. The alarm clock over on my desk said it was 4:38 a.m. I decided to go downstairs and have a bowl of cereal. I couldn't have done that a week earlier when I was still wrestling junior varsity at 113. I got used to being hungry. But now I sort of like the feeling of a well-fed stomach.

I didn't turn on any lights until I got down into the kitchen. I didn't want to wake up anybody else but I would have liked to have run the dream by Wheat. Then again, maybe I didn't. I'll admit the dream unsettled me. I hate when people not on our team are wrestling each other. I've had dreams like that before. I hate getting all those people in my head — wrestling around in there. I think I would rather go back to dreaming about me being in my underwear in English class.

While I was slurping down my Cheerios, I heard a car slow down and then the newspaper hit our porch. I decided to go out and get it. I knew there had been a Tribune reporter at the match because I had seen him talking to Coach Mathews right after we won. Usually, we only get the results published in tiny print in the paper — which is okay — but occasionally when there is a big meet like last night's, the paper will make a little bit of a deal of it.

I think a photographer was there, too. They usually only stay for the first couple of matches and so it's always the little guys who get their pictures in the paper. Big Jim sometimes grumbles about that. I grabbed the sports section and sure enough, there was a picture of Thirsty getting pinned and another one of Wheat holding her hand up in triumph. None of me struggling for my life, though, thank goodness.

I read the story and it made us sound pretty good. Wheat had a whole paragraph about her. I was mentioned with a couple other guys in a quote by Coach Mathews for coming up big — all because I didn't get pinned.

I was back in bed by 5:12 a.m. with the alarm ready to go off in 33 minutes. At least I wasn't going to have to fight off hunger on our morning run.

Dad had worked his part-time security job at the drug store over the weekend, so he told us after our meet that he was going to have to sleep in. He needed to catch up on his snoring. That was okay. I wanted to talk to Wheat, mainly about dreams but I'm sure Kelly Carson was going to come up.

"You're on the front page of the sports section," I told her as we climbed out of bed.

"What? You have ESP or something?" she said.

"I was up a little earlier. Some spooky dreams."

"Like dead people from next door?"

"No, like living people from our new lives."

"Poor little Billy Ray," Wheat said and then headed downstairs, already in her sweat clothes.

She took a quick look at the sports section that I had left on the kitchen counter and headed out the door. She was running in place on our front walk when I caught up with her.

"Here, your turn to wear it," she said as she tossed me the reflective vest that one of us always wears when Dad isn't with us.

Normally, he wears it but he insists that one of us don it when he isn't with us.

I hate to wear it. It makes me feel like a road sign. I understood the importance, though. During the school year, our early morning workouts are always in the dark and we usually run in the street, especially in the winter when the sidewalks can be slippery.

Although the temperature was below freezing, it didn't seem that bad. The wind wasn't blowing and the early morning sky was still showing the stars. I always like to look up and find the constellation of Orion — the only one I can easily identify because of his little belt and three-cornered cap. I usually call out to him, "Hi, Orion" even though I've never taken the time to look up who Orion was.

I was using socks on my hands because I hadn't been able to find my gloves during the last few days. The gloves don't match anyway, not that that's a big deal when your hands are cold.

My neck and shoulders hurt from my match the previous night and my legs are always stiff when I start on our runs. Wheat, meanwhile, looked as light-footed as an elf as we chugged along at about a seven-minute mile pace. We both had on hooded sweat shirts but I still had on a Chicago Cubs toboggan hat and Wheat wore pink earmuffs — my present to her this last Christmas.

After about a half mile of silence, Wheat finally said, "So how about your dreams last night. Anybody naked in them?"

"Nope," I said.

I didn't want to mention, though, that in most of my dreams I always seem to be in my underwear under some pretty embarrassing circumstances. I did tell her that I had been wrestling Kelly Carson and she was rooting for him to win. I also told her that Sally Guffie was beating up just about everyone who got near her, including Laurie Middlebrook.

"That's one messed-up mind you have, Spank. I'm not going to try to interpret them but I think that Big Jim's sister has more of a hold on you right now than Laurie Middlebrook does. You're a sad case."

"I think I liked being a nerd or a geek or the nobody that I was before all this social pressure and popularity came my way. And now do I have to worry about you and Kelly making moon eyes at each other?"

"There's nothing there. We were just doing a little peace making."

I didn't push it. Wheat had suddenly picked up the pace and it was getting hard to have any kind of conversation. She probably did that on purpose. We usually do a two-mile loop twice and we had just passed our house to start our third mile.

After a few minutes of silence, Wheat finally said, "Don't worry, Spank. After the formal and then the wrestling season, both you and I can probably go back into being nobodies."

"Yeah, and you say I sell myself short," I told her between breaths. "You are pretty and popular and a great wrestler."

"Popular? At least three-fourths of the population doesn't want to see a skinny little girl beat up on skinny little boys. Pretty? My hair goes in every direction but south and it doesn't help that I'm always in wrestling headgear. A great wrestler? Well, maybe that might be true someday but what's that going to get me down the road — cauliflower ears and a bent nose?"

She slowed down a little to catch her breath.

"Quit idolizing me, Spank. We all have our insecurities. You'll grow into a handsome, well-rounded man someday — if you let yourself — while I'll probably always be viewed as an untamable little wildcat until I have gray hair."

We both let that set in and then she let out a laugh. I followed.

"Purrrr, little wildcat," I said.

"And puke to you, Little Man," Wheat said in return.

I guess our deep thinking had run its course but I admitted to myself that I never really thought about Wheat as having any hang-ups on what her future might hold.

By that time we were back on our street, we were coming up on Mr. Saunders and Bootsie on their morning walk.

"Purrrr," said Wheat rather loudly as we skirted around them while back on a dry stretch of sidewalk.

"Oh, hazelnuts! You just took five years off my life!" Mr. Saunders yelled, obviously surprised by our presence. "And don't taunt my dog like that or I'll let him off his leash and he can have at your fast little feet!"

"Is that five years in a human's life or a dog's life?" Wheat shouted over her shoulder as we scurried on. "Gosh, he's starting to sound like the Wicked Witch of the West."

I actually like Mr. Saunders. He is usually pretty friendly when he isn't walking Bootsie. And I think he likes it when we give him a chance for some lively talk, faking a lot of his exasperation. I do think Bootsie would bite us, though, if Mr. Saunders did let him off the leash.

Back inside our house, Mom seemed ecstatic.

"What a great picture of you two on the front page of the paper!" she exclaimed.

Wait a minute, I thought. Wait one blood-sucking minute. I wasn't in the paper and I wouldn't want to be after my back was on the mat most of my match. "What do you mean the two of us?" I said.

Then she held up the front page of the paper — not the front of the sports page but the front page. And there on it was Big Jim hoisting Wheat in the air with a bunch of our teammates ready to swarm them. And off to their side, Sally was approaching me with her arms open and me looking like a little bunny about ready to be devoured by a wolf — a good-looking wolf — but a wolf nonetheless.

I hadn't even bothered to look at the front page when I brought in the paper earlier. I guess I should pay more attention to the real news.

"Wow," Ric — Dad — said as he came in the room and saw the front page held out by Mom. "I don't think I've ever seen a picture of a wrestling meet used on the front page. But I can see why. What a great shot of emotion and jubilation."

"It's absolutely precious," Mom added.

I don't think either Wheat or I would have used that word. I wondered what Laurie Middlebrook might think. And it wasn't like I had done something great or anything to be a part of this celebration picture.

But then I think Wheat had even stronger feelings about the picture than I did.

"It makes me look like I'm being tossed around like a little rag doll," she said. "I don't like it!"

"At least there's a picture of you in the sports section looking like a champion," I said to her. "I look like I'm about to be crushed by a crazed Amazon."

"Don't be silly," Mom said. "That's a picture that I want to order from the newspaper and have it framed."

She showed it to Lake in his high chair. "Ta-da," he said as Mom pointed to Wheat up in the air and hovering above everybody like an angel in flight. Then when she pointed to me, my little brother looked at me with a wide grin and said, "Spock."

That's as close as he has ever come to Spank.

"Yeah, maybe that should be my new name," I said. "My ears will probably look like Spock's if they keep getting dragged across a mat as much as they were last night."

Lake studied the paper a little more and then said, "Spock" again. If only I could stay as cool as the universe's most famous Vulcan during the next few days.

Spock. Like I said, Wheat and I seem to attract nicknames. And I think that people who are either really big like Big Jim or people who are small like us are the ones who get stuck with the most aliases. I guess that isn't always bad.

CHAPTER 16

I wasn't looking forward all that much to our drive to school.

"So maybe this is the time that Sally will want to get in the backseat with you," Wheat said as we waited for Big Jim to pull up in front of our house.

Like I was going to let that comment pass.

"Well, maybe Big Jim will hold you out his window with one hand like a little trophy. Or maybe he could use you as a hood ornament. How about we don't say anything about the picture and maybe they won't either?"

Wheat nodded and then mumbled, "These are the times when I wish I was in the science club instead of on the wrestling team."

"Yeah, your weird buddy Paul from your biology class would like that," I said.

When we did get picked up, neither of the Guffies mentioned the front-page picture. Big Jim still seemed a little aglow after winning the decisive match the previous night. I think I even smelled some after-shave on him although it could have been Sally upping her perfume potency.

That reminded me that I didn't think Wheat had used her Midnight Breeze for her match the previous night. I decided I would ask about that later.

Sally was actually quite complimentary, not only to me and Wheat but to her big brother as well. I was trying hard to see if she was being genuine or not. If she wasn't, then she was doing a pretty good job of acting. I'll have to say that her bear hug after the meet had seemed genuine. It just about cracked my ribs.

Before we got out of the car, I finally asked what Big Jim and Sally had thought about the pictures in the paper.

"What pictures?" Big Jim said. "Our parents only get the newspaper on the weekend."

That explained a lot. They were curious and I said they should probably get a copy or look at the paper's website. Wheat didn't say anything. After Big Jim parked in the student lot, it was kind of awkward when we all got out. Big Jim always heads for the gym for his first class — advanced weight training, an elective — and I didn't know whether I should walk in with Wheat or Sally. Fortunately, Sally saw some of her friends and hailed them down.

"Let's go Spock," Wheat said.

"Aye, aye, Captain. I'll beam both of us into school," I said and followed her down the sidewalk.

———

I did get a few comments over the course of the day. Our win over Mishawaka was the big news during our principal's morning announcements. Mr. Rammel, our algebra teacher, even had Wheat and I stand up to the applause of our fellow students.

When we sat down, Bobby Taylor nudged me from his desk across from me and whispered, "I thought you lost."

"Yeah, but I lost in magnificent fashion," I said.

When I took off for biology class, I saw Kelly Carson coming down the hallway. I had never seen him during this particular break between classes and I'm not sure he even saw me as he passed. Of course, there were a lot of kids in the hall. I forced myself not to look back. I had a creepy feeling that I might see Wheat waiting for him.

After lunch and just before English class, Bobby caught up with me and said, "Do you think Laurie Middlebrook knows you lost in magnificent fashion?"

I hoped she did but I also hoped she didn't see the newspaper in the morning. I don't think many high school kids look at it. Just getting dressed and brushing your teeth are hard enough for most kids to do and still make it to school on time without stretching out the paper in front of them at the breakfast table. But then Laurie's dad is the mayor and so …

"I saw you in the paper this morning, Spank," Laurie said as soon as I walked into Mrs. Murphy's door. "That must have been really exciting. I wish I could have been there. You didn't wrestle Sally Guffie after the meet, did you? It looks like she was about ready to attack you."

"If she had, I would have probably lost," I admitted. "I think she was heading for her brother to hug him and I happened to be in her way."

That seemed to satisfy her.

"You looked cute in your wrestling uniform. My dad showed me the picture this morning."

"What did he think?"

"I'm not sure. I still think he might have the wrong idea about you. Maybe about all boys that come into my life. I don't know. I'm working on him, though."

One guy in the whole town of South Bend thinks I'm a roughneck and it happens to be the mayor — and the father of the girl who still remains No. 1 on my dream list. I would have to say, though, that Sally Guffie has gone from about No. 9,203 to the Top 5 over the course of a week. And she seemed to be getting close to knocking Mrs. Riley out of the No. 2 spot. Of course, if Elle Fanning was a few inches shorter, I would have her No. 2.

I'm sure that Mrs. Murphy, who is not on my list, doesn't know anything about wrestling — or even sports, for that matter — but she gave me a quick look and said, "Billy Ray apparently had a big evening last night. Let's see if he included reading the O. Henry short story I assigned all of you. Would you give me a synopsis of 'A Reformed Reformation.'"

Yikes! I had only skimmed it after our meet. But I knew the story already. I had done a report on it in junior high and if has always been one of my favorites. In the story, Jimmy Valentine is a safe cracker who eventually goes straight but then has to make up his mind if he wants to leave a kid trapped in a safe and protect his past identity or save the kid and probably go to jail. I love that name, Jimmy Valentine, and I think that's partly why I remember the story so well.

I could talk about Jimmy Valentine anytime and I stood up and faced the class matter-of-factly while I explained it. I do think that wrestling has given me a lot more self-confidence even if I had been beaten, 11-3, in my last match.

"Both brains and brawn," Mrs. Murphy said as I sat down.

I blushed. I felt a little guilty, though, that I had barely reviewed it the night before. Who knew she was going to single me out?

After class, I started to walk Laurie down the hall but she found some friends she seemed to need to talk to. That was okay with me even though it seemed to be a bit of a brush-off. Even though I might be madly in love with her, I'm just happy that she seems to like me, even if it's just a little. She might be a little jealous of Sally Guffie, too. You just never know when it comes to love and war — or so I've heard when Mom watches those movies on the Hallmark Channel.

Then again, maybe she saw I lost, 11-3, and didn't understand that I was still a hero — ha, ha — by keeping from getting pinned.

Bobby Taylor, who probably hasn't been all that happy that I've been walking with Laurie instead of him, came up to me.

"Got a question, Spank," he said.

I hoped it wasn't going to be about girls.

"Fire away," I said.

"If you had been Jimmy Valentine in that story and Kelly Carson was in the safe, do you think you would have let him out?"

"Probably," I said. "But if he was stuck in one of our lockers with those little breathing holes up at the top, I might have left him in there until the end of the day."

Before practice later that afternoon, we were messing around and having a pretty good time when we should have been doing our pushups and sit-ups. Dion Borden suggested that Big Jim and Wheat re-enact their little scene at the end of the meet that made the paper. But Wheat balked.

"I'm not playing around," she growled when Dion put his hand on her shoulder like she should go along with his suggestion since he was a captain.

She shrugged it off and then continued, "We've got three days until the conference meet and you guys are acting like a bunch of giggling girls, sorry to say. We should pretend that we just got our butts beat and are looking for revenge. I know the Mishawaka wrestlers are doing that right now and we barely beat them. This is the worst of times for us to get a little soft in our preparation."

By that time, Coach Mathews had come out of his office.

"Well, I guess there's nothing else I need to say," he said. "I think Tanda has pretty much covered it all. Now, let's get to it."

And so we did. Dion or Big Jim, our senior captains, probably should have given that sort of speech. But then Wheat, even though a scrawny sophomore and a girl to boot, has probably become the unofficial leader of our team.

I was glad she spoke up and I sure didn't want Big Jim to do their acrobat act again. I figured that somebody would want to pretend to be Sally Guffie and put me in a bear hug for the second act.

I made sure I paired off with Wheat and Dion and Doug Littlejohn as much as I could while avoiding Thirsty and The Torso. I wanted to really work hard on my moves so I could be respectable at the conference meet. Benny Goodchild was getting over his toe injury and was showing up to practice and helping me out with some advice.

I liked that. Benny knows wrestling pretty well. He's a student of the sport but not the toughest guy in the gym. Sometimes, a good technician can beat a tough guy. But then if the tough guy is a good technician as well, an opponent like Benny is going to be dead meat.

Even if he hadn't messed up his toe, I think I could have handled him by now. Just saying. Not trying to brag. I have gotten better and I think I could even give Wheat a pretty good match now that I have a few more pounds on me.

CHAPTER 17

When I'm old and gray — or bald like Dad, even though he shaves a good deal of his hair — I figure that Thursday will probably be considered the craziest day of my life. At least I hope so. I don't think I could go through many days like that.

It started out a little unsettling when Dad knocked on the bathroom door and came in with a disposable razor and shaving cream. "It's time you learned to shave, Spank," he said.

I knew I had been cultivating a little bit of what Dad calls peach fuzz on my chin, but I thought I would let it go for a while and see if it might eventually develop into a little bit of stubble. It seems like half the younger actors in the movies have some kind of facial hair. And look at all the athletes who are sporting beards these days. It seems to work for them. Why not me?

And I was halfway insulted, halfway embarrassed that Dad would even want to get involved in my facial makeup. He had never commented on my occasional zit, one of them taking up about half my forehead not that long ago.

"What about if I want to cultivate a little five-o'clock shadow?" I said.

"You probably won't have a true five-o'clock shadow for at least five more years," he said. "I just think this would be a good time to look like a young man who wants to take care of his looks before a big thing like his first dance. And besides, you can always grow it back."

I was about ready to tell him that it took me 15 years to grow my little bit of peach fuzz but decided to let it go.

So just to get him off my back, I let him show me how to apply the shaving cream and how to take nice steady strokes.

"And first and foremost, always drench your face with hot water — as hot as you can stand — and wipe off the blade after each stroke with hot water. Hot water is even more important than the sharpness of your blade."

And so off my peach fuzz came. I wondered if anybody would even notice. When I was done and admiring my smooth face in the mirror, Dad gave me one more tip.

"Never let your sister — or any woman — use your razor on her legs," he said. "Leg hair dulls a blade so badly that it would be like shaving with a piece of glass."

Did Wheat shave her legs? I had never seen her do so. Was Dad just assuming that?

I asked her as we put our books in our backpacks and got ready for school. "Of course I do," she said. "I've been doing it for a year, not that it is any of your business. And I shave my armpits, too."

Yucko! Too much information.

But I was surprised I didn't know that, as close as we are. I guess I always thought that the razor blades were Mom's. And to be honest, I don't think I even knew that girls grew hair under their arms. Maybe women, but not girls. I have to admit I've never seen armpit hair in a girl before.

I was thinking about all that when Wheat said, "Smooth face, Spank."

"What are you talking about?" I asked.

"You minus the little cat whiskers on your chinny-chin-chin," she answered.

"Were you listening in on Dad and me?"

"Didn't have to. I'm the one who told him to give you the shaving lesson."

That's when I started thinking that a bigger house and an extra bathroom might not be a bad idea.

"Now you have a reason to use some nice-smelling after-shave lotion," Wheat added. "A lot of girls supposedly like it."

"I'm not ready for this," was all I could say.

I certainly wasn't ready for the bombshell that Laurie dropped on me later in the day. She had asked me in English class if I could meet her right after school for something important. I told her I couldn't be late for wrestling practice but she said it wouldn't take long. We could meet out in front of the school on one of the benches.

She was there first and sitting with a couple of her girl friends. When they saw me coming, the friends got up and one of them said, "We'll see you at the car, Laurie." I think her friend's name is Tara. She looked back at me like I had a worm coming out of my nose.

Laurie, meanwhile, looked at me a little nervously.

"Oh, Spank," she said as I sat down beside her. "I'm going to have to ask you if it's okay if we break our date to the formal. I'm so sorry."

How can you feel overwhelming disappointment as well as a little relief at the same time?

"Why?" I asked.

"David Butcher just got home from Army boot camp and my dad insists I go with him. His parents and my parents are best friends and even though he's three years older them me, David and I have always been close. I've been writing to him but I didn't think he would be home for another week."

I didn't have anything to say and so she continued.

"I like you a lot, Spank, and hope we stay friends. And if you really want me to go with you, I still will. It will just be really awkward with my dad. I don't know why he is being like that. Being mayor, I guess, he's used to getting his way. He's put the guilt trip on me by saying that David needs some fun and normalcy in his life during this little break from his training. And that he's serving our country and might be sent overseas sometime soon. I guess he's lost about 15 pounds."

I didn't say anything or ask which weight class he might now be in. Fifteen pounds would put me even with Thirsty and Laurie probably wouldn't have asked me to the dance in the first place.

While she was waiting for me to let her off the hook, I thought I would give her my own version of a guilt trip. I just sat there. After a few seconds, I guess she sort of figured out what I was doing because she started sniffling. Oh, boy.

"I understand," I finally said. "It was a privilege to be asked by you. You've got my permission to go with David Whoever."

"David Butcher," she said. "He's a great guy, just like you. I'm not in love with him or anything — at least not now — but my parents seem to be in love with him. He's always been a bit of a favorite of theirs. That's maybe why my dad didn't warm up to you or Kelly. It probably had nothing to do with your fight. He's the first boy I ever kissed. It's just really awkward. I wish I wasn't even on the formal's court and had to go!"

At that point, another one of her friends — I think she's another Tara — came from the parking lot and yelled, "Laurie, we need to go."

I didn't know if that had been planned or not, but I was ready to get going, too. Laurie stood and so did I.

She actually gave me a peck on my cheek and said, "Thanks so much for understanding, Spank. I owe you. I know you don't deserve this."

I nodded and she started to walk away.

"Hey, Laurie," I yelled to her. "Tell your dad I probably won't vote for him when I turn 18."

She laughed. "That's one of the reasons I like you, Spank. You're always so funny."

I figured it wouldn't do me any good telling her I wasn't meaning to be funny. Her dad didn't impress me that much anyway. I don't even know if he is a Republican or a Democrat. But when I find out, I'll probably become the other.

Wheat, who seemed to appear out of nowhere, gave me a nudge.

"What's up, Romeo. It looks like you upset your darling."

"She just saved me the cost of a corsage," I said.

"Oh, Spank. I'm sorry."

"Not to worry. I can now concentrate on the conference meet and maybe even try to win a match or two."

"Why did she back out?"

"Old flame — three years older than her — is coming back from Army boot camp earlier than expected. Who knows, maybe he's deserting. She probably wants to go with him but she's using her dad as an excuse. Oh, well. I'm okay with it. I just hope Mom doesn't get too upset. I'm sure she'll get over it almost as quickly as I do."

"Did she let some tears flow for the right effect?"

"Yep."

"Figures. You know, Spank, I liked Laurie when we got together with her last week. I think she's a pretty good person overall even though she probably expects everything to go her way. She's just different than us right now in some ways. It may not be that way when we all get a little older and we don't have to worry about what our parents and high school friends think. I know she didn't mean to hurt you but she probably could have handled this better. But, hey, we're all just 15 years old. We all have a lot to learn yet."

"That all sounds like a comment from one of those advice columns, Wheat. But you're right. Maybe when Laurie is 19 or 20 years old, she'll look back at me as the one who got away."

"Come on, little fishy, let's go get some mat burns."

Practice went fine, all things considered. Nothing like putting all your energy into beating someone else in a wrestling workout than worrying about feeling sorry for yourself. Benny Goodchild was back in uniform and obviously trying to win his spot back at 120. I wasn't going to let that happen. I wrestled about as well as I ever have at practice, even pinning Doug Littlejohn at one point.

When we squared off to do some takedown drills at the end of practice, Tommy the Torso actually made sure he paired off with Wheat instead of me. He normally hates to wrestle Wheat but I guess he noticed I had things going.

Big Jim gave us a ride home and mentioned that he really liked the dance class on Monday. He even said that he and Sally had demonstrated some of the steps to their mom.

"First time I've ever got that close to my sister since I tried to strangle her for rubbing deep heating rub in my underpants a couple of years ago," he said.

"She's a good dancer," I said, filling in the conversation gap since Big Jim seemed a little embarrassed about what he had just revealed.

"She says the same about you, Spank," he said. "It's really creepy how nice she's been acting recently. I know our grandma has a lot to do with it but I think you've been a good influence on her, Spank. You're too normal than what is usually her type. I don't know if she really likes you or not, but she seems to enjoy ... well, I guess it's flirting a little with you. And she's been halfway bearable to be around lately. Usually, she likes guys a little more … macho. No offense."

"None taken," I said. "People change. Look at me. A year ago, I was maybe the biggest wimp in school. And now, I don't even think I would make the Top 10 list — or is that the Bottom 10?"

"Oh, brother," Wheat said somewhat disgustedly as Big Jim pulled up in front of our house and let us off.

"What's the big news?" Dad asked as we walked in the front door.

"I'm a free agent again," I said. "I'm not going to the dance with Laurie after all. Her dad must have noticed I was on some Most Wanted list down at the post office."

"Whhhaaaattt?" came Mom's screech from the kitchen.

"I've got to go to the bathroom," I said to Wheat. "You want to fill her in? I'm not in the mood to go through the story again."

"Will do," she said and headed for the kitchen.

Dad hung around.

"You want to talk about it, Spank?"

"Naaa. I really do have to go to the bathroom," I said as I headed upstairs. "You can listen to Wheat, too. She can explain it better than I can."

"Okay," Dad said. "I'm available any time, though."

After the first three steps, I turned and said, "Winter formal or not, at least I know how to shave properly now."

Dad nodded.

"How about our next man-to-man talk being about tying a good Windsor knot?"

We both laughed. We both hate ties. I was glad that I got to kid with him and that Wheat had the job of consoling Mom. I think this was one of those times that I was glad I had started calling Ric by Dad. That's what he is, after all. I'm sorry I lost my real dad and Ric won't replace him. He'll just be my second dad — and I'm a lucky guy for it.

At dinner— lasagna — nobody mentioned the formal although Mom was looking at me in a woeful way. I think woeful was a good word for it. Wheat must have persuaded her to keep her mouth shut about it. I know it was hard for Mom. She wants sort of a fairytale life for me after what happened to us. Come to think about it, my life has turned a little fairytale-ish on me lately. Call me Cinder-fella. Just don't call me Little Man — ha, ha.

Thank goodness for Lake to keep the mood from being too dreary around the table. He kept pointing to me and saying "Spock," apparently his new word for the week. Then he would point at Wheat and say, "Ta-da." Then some strange sounds came from his high chair and he went, "Uh-oh." Really, I'm not exaggerating. The kid is a poop machine.

Mom scooped him up and took him up for a diaper change. Then a cell phone rang. It was coming from Wheat's direction. She reached into her pocket, looked at who was calling and excused herself.

I got up to follow her when Dad said, "Oh, no, you don't, buddy. I'm not going to get stuck with all these dishes. You clear and clean off the counters and I'll load the dish washer. I think you should know by now that kids your age don't like an audience when they get a phone call."

He was right, of course. So we went to work. Ric takes a lot of pride in his dish washing. He worked in the kitchen of a restaurant when he was growing up on the south side of Chicago and he said he always liked cleaning the dishes. He grew up a little poor and he said his family didn't always have the hottest of water.

I guess I believe him. He also said he always liked getting his hands clean in the hot-soapy water and also seeing a mess turn into neat stack of dishes.

I can't say that I feel the same as he does about doing the dishes but he makes it fun when we do them together. He usually flicks water at me and sometimes I'll toss the dishes for him to catch if Mom isn't around.

When we were finishing up, Wheat came back in the room and looked all serious like. "Dad, do you mind if I go to Mug and Munchies in a little while to meet a friend?"

"What friend?" Dad and I asked at the same time.

"Kelly Carson," she mumbled.

"Who?" Dad and I asked together again although we both heard her well enough.

"Kelly Carson," Wheat almost shouted. "You heard me. Spank knows he gave me a ride to school the other day and he's walked me to a couple of classes. He felt bad about what happened last week. If Spank can go to a big dance with the mayor's daughter — oops, would have gone — can't I have a coke with a guy? Don't worry, Dad, he already knows I can whip him. And he knows you're a cop."

"I don't like him," I blurted out.

"You don't know him, Spank." Wheat blurted back.

Dad stayed quiet for a moment.

"I don't know this guy except that he is a good athlete and that he drives a car that's a little too fast for a kid his age. And I wasn't exactly impressed with the way he was acting when I got to The Mug last week."

"He sort of humiliated himself, I'll admit, Dad," Wheat sort of pleaded. "You've always been big about giving people second chances and I've done that with Kelly. He hasn't disappointed so far."

"I don't like this, Dad," I huffed.

"It's none of your business," Wheat said. "I've been okay with your first excursion with the opposite sex. So let me be. Bug out."

Dad seemed amused. I wasn't. I didn't know if I was mad that Kelly was trying to move in on my sister on that she hadn't told me all about it.

"I'll tell you what," Dad finally said. "You can go, Wheat, but you'll be taking a chaperone along just like Spank did last week with the mayor's daughter. You can either pick me, in my full uniform and my firearm at my side, or Spank with his new clean-shaven face. Your choice."

"You mean you don't trust me enough to meet him by myself?"

"Oh, I trust you, all right," he said. "I'm just not sure I'm ready to trust this Kelly Carson yet."

"I'm not going," I said.

"Oh, yes, you are," Wheat said. "You can sit up at the counter but you're going. I don't think a Coke date needs a police presence."

I stormed out of the kitchen, but I felt Dad's long arm of the law on my shoulder before I hit the stairs. He must have moved pretty quick despite his sore knee.

"I need you on this, Spank," he said. "I'm a father and I worry about my kids, especially a daughter no matter how tough she is. You're the one person in the whole world I would trust with the welfare of that little girl in the other room. And you and your Mom are the best gifts I've ever received. I might not always show it, but

I'm a worry wart when it comes to my three kids. So please go with her so I don't have to and really screw up the night for her."

His words had hit my heart dead-center. I gave him a nod and he gave me a quick man hug. I was fighting back some tears when Wheat walked into the living room.

"What did you do, Dad?" she asked. "Spank the Spanker?"

"When we going?" is all I asked.

"Twenty minutes. Wipe your tears, girly boy."

Dad grabbed us both and gave us a group hug. Mom was coming down the stairs while holding Lake. "Meeee," he said. So we included the two of them in our hug even though neither one of them knew what it was about.

"By the way," Dad said. "Loosey Goosey, Lake and I are going to sneak out real quick and take another look at that house we're all a little interested in."

CHAPTER 18

We could feel a bit of a winter thaw as Wheat and I headed off to Mug and Munchies — or just The Mug as Dad apparently calls it. He says a lot of the cops have coffee there in the morning. They pretty much leave it as a hangout for us kids in the evening.

Without verbalizing it, I think Wheat and I decided to let some things left unsaid for a while. It was one of the few times when it seemed a little awkward for us to share our feelings with each other.

The temperature was in the low 40s and most of the snow had melted. It was a little too early for spring to be in the air. I wouldn't have been able to smell it anyway.

"I thought you only used that Midnight Breeze for worthy opponents," I finally said.

"Is it that strong?" Wheat asked, sounding alarmed.

"It will fade by the time we get there," I assured her. "The wind will blow it all over the neighborhood and everyone will fall in love with each other tonight."

"I swear to the Almighty, Spank. If you keep it up, I'll plant your face in a snowdrift right now and make you squeal like a little piggie before I let you up. You want to cry like a baby twice in one evening?"

"Okay, okay, I just had to say something. I'm done now. Let's get this over with. I'm just here because Dad wants to make sure you drink Diet Coke instead of regular and that you don't nibble on any fries. Big meet in two days, remember?"

We went back to silence until she said, "I like that you're calling Dad Dad. I know it was easier for me to call Mom Mom. DeeDee falls far short in comparison. But your real dad sounded like a pretty good guy. I just feel happy you and Dad seem to have gotten a lot closer over the last year or so."

"He's always been good to me," I answered. "You know I got teased a little that a big black dude was suddenly my father. Maybe I was a little embarrassed how different we were — and maybe a little jealous that I had to share Mom. But he never tried to make me do macho things or even make me feel that I had to pretend to be tough. He's a great guy and I love him. Heck, I even like you a little, too."

"Okay, okay, let's don't get gushy," she said and we let that subject drop.

I glanced over at Wheat and she looked a little nervous. She also looked downright pretty — her hair curled nicely and what looked like a little makeup around her dark eyes. I wasn't going to say anything about that. I figured I already got away with my one shot for the night about the Midnight Breeze.

Kelly's Mustang was parked outside The Mug — I think I'll also start calling it that although I do like the Mug and Munchies alliteration.

"He was going to pick me up but I told him that you were coming, too, and that a walk would do us good," Wheat said. "I'm not sure Dad would have let me ride with him anyway, although I already did the other morning."

Boy, did I feel funny walking in there. I saw Kelly sitting in a booth smiling like a dork. I walked over to the counter and sat down. But he yelled at me to come over, too. Tony the Cook came out from the kitchen — I think Jenny the Waitress may have said something to him. He looked me over and then over at the table where Wheat had just sat down across the Kelly.

"Am I going to have to set up a demilitarized zone between you guys?" he asked.

"What's that?" I asked.

"Never mind," Tony said. "Just tell me that all of you got your orneriness out of your systems the other night."

The three of us nodded. Even a couple of kids in another booth nodded, too, probably just in case Tony was including them. Then he chuckled and looked directly at Wheat.

"You're that little girl who's whipping all those boys in wrestling, aren't you?"

Wheat nodded.

"Well then, no charge tonight. I'm a big fan of little heroes — or heroines if that's the better word. Just refrain from beating up the boys in here, okay?"

"Thanks," Wheat said. "We're just having Cokes — mine a diet."

"Speak for yourself," I said. "If it's free, I'm having a hamburger."

"We just ate," Wheat protested.

"And I'm going to keep eating until I make 120 pounds," I said.

"If you're going to be a glutton, maybe you should go back to the counter," Wheat added.

"Are you guys always this edgy?" Tony the Cook said. "Jenny will be over to take your orders. I'll tell her it's on me as long as there's no fisticuffs."

Kelly was just sitting there and listening to all this.

Finally, Wheat looked at him and said, "Well, what do you think?"

"I think I'll have a hamburger, too," he said with a smile. "My mom made some kind of Chinese dish tonight and I didn't like it at all."

"Well, that's one thing that you and the Spanker have in common," Wheat said. "I might have to look a little harder to find other things."

"Well, let's see," Kelly said. "Favorite sports team?"

"Cubs," I said.

"Well, what do you know? We agree on that. Favorite singer?"

"Miranda Lambert."

"I'm not really into country. Mine would probably be Dirty Honey. Favorite teacher?"

"Mr. Rammel."

"We're way off on that one," Kelly said. "He gave me a C last year and kept me off the honor roll. Mine would be Mrs. Kern, my English teacher."

That surprised me. She must be about 70 years old and looks about 100.

"What about Mrs. Riley?"

Kelly looked a little embarrassed.

"Nice to look at, but Mrs. Kern really got me into liking literature."

"Does it always have to be about looks with you, Spank?" Wheat cut in. "I think Kelly is looking at it in a much more mature manner."

I felt like saying that we wouldn't be sitting across from him if Wheat looked like Winnie the Pooh instead of one of the prettiest girls at Clay High.

Jenny the Waitress, a Clay senior, came over then and took our orders. After that, it seemed that I was a persona non grata — I'm sure Kelly learned what that means from Mrs. Kern — as Kelly and Wheat began talking about what they liked and didn't like.

I'll have to say, though; it was pretty interesting to listen to them. Kelly said he didn't really like football all that much but was pretty good at it and his dad would go into deep depression if he gave it up. His favorite sport was baseball and he was worried that a dislocated thumb he suffered in the last football game of the season might hurt his grip on the ball.

The Mustang he drove was really his older sister's, but she had gotten a couple of speeding tickets at college and their dad had taken it away from her for at least the rest of her sophomore year.

He admitted he had dyslexia and it had really made him struggle in school until it was diagnosed. That's why he really liked reading now and why Mrs. Kern was his favorite teacher.

Of course, he wanted to be a major-league baseball player but knew that would be a long shot. As a kid, he always wanted to be a fire fighter and he still thought that would be a worthy profession.

Wheat went through some of her likes and dislikes that I had already heard a thousand times — yada, yada, yada. But then she said that she might like to be a nurse and I had never heard her mention that before.

And then Kelly turned to me and asked me if I had any life goals.

"To be 6-foot-3 and weigh about 220 pounds," I answered.

That made him laugh. I was starting to have a hard time working up a strong dislike for Kelly. I wasn't crazy about how he was looking at my sister, though. But I wasn't crazy about how my sister was kind of goo-goo eyeing him, either. Then I noticed that Jenny the Waitress was kind of giving him the same look. It must be tough to be that handsome.

I almost asked him about that until he said, "Tanda told me why you're not going to the winter formal with Laurie. I hope this doesn't break your bubble, but that's the same reason we broke up — although we had only been dating four months. She told me she couldn't go to the formal with me if David Butcher was back in town. I guess he's going to be back, huh? That's more her dad than her. Nutty guy and yet he's our mayor. I'm surprised Laurie is as normal as she is."

That explained a lot. I wasn't even Plan B with Laurie but Plan C — or worse. I decided not to tell Kelly that Laurie said she would only dump me if Tom Holland, alias Spiderman, called.

But I couldn't help myself.

"So who are you going to go to the formal with, Kelly?"

"Spank!" Wheat almost shrieked.

"Well, I asked your sister but she said she was planning on being in the championship match of the conference meet. So I may go watch her. The winter formal is more of a senior class thing anyway."

I kept going.

"Rumor has it Sally Guffie was expecting you to ask her."

"Spank!" Wheat said even louder and I saw Tony the Cook look out the little window from the kitchen.

Kelly laughed.

"Sally and I have a complicated relationship. We've known each other since we were little kids. Our parents even have pictures of us in the bathtub together — I could probably blackmail her with that one. We're buds, more like brother and sister, and it always took both of us to handle Big Jim, who never has been too keen on me. Sally and I were always the ones who played together. We're pretty protective of one another. We just don't advertise it. So, yeah, we could go to some things together if one of us was desperate for a date. But it would be more out of friendship.

"As pretty as she is," Kelly continued, "she doesn't fare that well with boys — the nice ones seem intimidated and the bad ones don't go to dances or make it past her dad's inspection. She's never really had a steady. And I'm thinking she might not get asked to the winter formal at this late date. I don't think it bothers that much."

"You would probably look like Ken and Barbie together," I said.

That was it for Wheat. She punched me in the ribs, probably harder than she should have since I, too, had the biggest meet of my life ahead of me.

"Easy, Tanda," Kelly said. "I guess he might be right. Sally definitely could be Barbie. Me Ken? I'm hoping not. But, yeah, maybe some people would look at us that way. I need to get a nice scar or something. Or maybe have somebody like Big Jim flatten my nose."

If my ribs weren't hurting so much, I figured that this would be a good time to ask him why he was a bit of a bully to me recently. And why he thought he needed to act like such a jerk the last time we were all at The Mug.

I think he saw me stewing a little. Maybe he even read my mind.

"I know you probably don't like me much. I probably wouldn't if I were you, either. I was just showing off a little when I banged you into the lockers. That was pretty immature of me."

"That wasn't any big deal," I said. "First time Mrs. Riley ever gave me a second look."

"I have not heard about that," Wheat cut in.

We both ignored her.

"But what happened here last week was inexcusable. I had no idea that you guys and Laurie were going to be in here. I sort of lost it a little to see Laurie probably leading on somebody else. It really bugged me. I reacted badly."

"You didn't fare so well, either," I couldn't help but say.

Kelly smiled at that.

"Tanda pretty much gave me what I had coming. But it was you who almost knocked me out with that punch of yours."

"It was my head," I said. "I lost my balance and fell into you and my head sort of became a torpedo, I guess."

"Then you have one really hard head," he chuckled.

"And all this time I thought you hit him with some kind of roundhouse punch," Wheat said. "That explains a lot. I should have guessed that."

We all laughed and talked about a lot of different stuff after that. I could tell that there were some sparks between Wheat and Kelly and I still wasn't so sure how I felt about that. At least I felt a little better about Kelly — maybe not yet great, but better.

I didn't know if Wheat's Midnight Breeze was wafting over to the other side of the booth, but I was definitely getting a good whiff.

"You like my sister's perfume," I said before I could stop myself.

"Very nice," Kelly said as he watched Wheat rummage through her purse that she hardly ever carried.

"Yeah, it's called Midnight Breeze ..." I started just as she sprayed me in the face with that mantrap of a scent.

That did it. I picked up my Coke and moved back to the counter to wait for my hamburger. Now and then, I would look over at the two of them and they obviously couldn't care less if I was in the same establishment.

It had been me who had at least been grazed by one of Cupid's arrows last week and now it looked like it was these two with the same problem. Who would have guessed? Not me.

CHAPTER 19

Kelly drove us home. I sat in the back, of course. It doesn't matter who's in a car with me. If there are more than two people, I always end up in the back. I was so little as a kid that I had to sit on a booster seat in the back until I was in the fourth grade. And people must assume that little guys prefer the backseat — in the middle of it if there are five people. Far from true, of course. I dream about sitting shotgun with the window open and the wind blowing through my short hair.

I can't wait for driver's education in the summer. It may be the only way I will ever get to sit in the front seat.

As we approached the funeral home, I suddenly remembered that I had told Todd Dixon that I would push the snow out back.

"Let me out in front of the funeral home," I said to Kelly. "I need to clear the snow off their basketball court."

"They have a basketball court?" Kelly asked in an unbelieving way.

"Yeah, the spirits from inside there like to come out and play at night," I replied. "Ask Wheat. She watches them through our bedroom window."

"Spank!" she yelled yet another time.

And then I remembered. I said "our" bedroom window. That's something that both of us don't want anyone to know about, especially somebody like Kelly. He didn't seem to notice, though. He seemed too interested in the fact that a funeral home had a basketball court.

"I want to see this basketball court," he said.

"Okay by me," I said. "Pull into the driveway on the left there and it will take you around."

He did and I was happy to see that most of the snow had melted off because of the warmer weather. I would be able to push the snow off rather than lift it. Easy money.

"This is pretty neat back here," Kelly said. "I'll help you clear the snow and then I'll take you on in a game of Horse."

A game of Horse didn't appeal to me much since a basketball might as well be a bowling ball the way I shoot. But I would let Kelly man a snow shovel if he wanted to show Wheat what a good guy he was.

"I'll get the shovels," I said.

I put in the combination to the garage where the Dixon brothers keep the coach and limousine. It's also where the snow shovels are kept and where a few basketballs are usually rolling around.

I've washed the two vehicles on occasion, too. The limousine is for the dead person's family and the coach is for the dearly departed. The coach used to be called a hearse but that must have become too creepy of a name for some people. So you don't hardly hear it called that anymore. As you can see, I'm getting this funeral home stuff down pat. Nope, no interest in being a funeral director when I grow up, though. Being in the prep room pretty much convinced me of that.

A few times, I have even backed both vehicles out of the garage so I could wash them. One time, the radio came on when I started the coach and a singer named James Brown yelled out, "I feel good!" I doubt anybody whoever rode in the back would have agreed. Then again, maybe they would have.

When I was putting in the combination, I suddenly realized that Kelly was right behind me. "I've never been in a funeral home at night," he said. "I bet it would be spookier than a haunted house."

I'm not going to lie to you. I once took Bobby Taylor inside on a dare. He said I was too chicken to take him inside. I was shocked myself when I saw a body in the viewing room, apparently still there after an earlier visitation. When Bobby saw the body illuminated by the one light left on, he didn't look all that good.

He went skedaddling out of there and never mentioned the funeral home again. I felt a little guilty about sneaking in there with him that time but I didn't feel so bad that Bobby had the pants scared off him that night.

I didn't even think about taking Kelly in, though

"You want a tour?" I said, sort of sarcastically.

"What's all in there?" he asked.

"A couple of viewing rooms, some offices, a roomful of caskets and a kitchen upstairs along with a prep room."

"Are there any bodies?"

"Don't know. Maybe in the prep room upstairs. Sometimes, there is a body in one of the viewing rooms if they have him or her ready for a funeral the next day."

"What about us going in?" Kelly asked.

I looked at Wheat who was still hovering around the car about 40 feet away. She didn't want any part of this. In fact, I was a little surprised that she even let Kelly drive her around to the back of the funeral home. I knew she was having the woolies. Served her right for getting involved with Kelly.

So I said to him, "I'll tell you what. If you can persuade Wheat to come in with us, I'll let you get in in one of the caskets. How about that? Maybe I'll even close it on you for a second. You can pretend you're Dracula."

He grinned and walked back over to Wheat. I was smirking because no way was he going to talk my sister into going in there at night. No way. She might be half African-American and half of a lot of Pacific Islands but she would be whiter than me after venturing inside a funeral home. No way.

While they talked, I put up the garage door and got the funeral home's big shovels. I also kicked a basketball outside. Wheat was shaking her head and then, all of a sudden, I heard her say, "Oh, okay."

"Okay what?" I said.

"Okay, she said she would go in with us if we don't get near any dead bodies and she can close you in a casket, too," Kelly answered.

Hmmmm.

"What's the turnaround here, Sis?" I said. "You would never even think about going in there before."

Of course, I knew what it was no matter what she said. Kelly had the charm, even on an apparent boy-buster like Wheat.

"Kelly said he would give me a driving lesson in his Mustang," she said. "And you act so brave around here, Spank. I want to see you get in a casket. But no way do we get around any dead people. If we do, Spank, there will be one more body in there and Benny Goodchild and his bad toe and all will be wrestling at 120 in the conference meet."

I just shook my head in disbelief, deciding not to mention that the Mustang was really Kelly's sister's car.

"Then if we're going to do this, Kelly, you need to move your car out from back here and somewhere down the block. Then again, why don't you let Wheat drive it over to our house for her first lesson and maybe Dad will be looking out the window. That would work out swell for both of you."

"Shut up, Spank," was her reply.

While they were moving the car, I quickly started pushing the snow off the basketball court. By the time the two love birds came back, I was about done. Kelly did help finish up, though.

The garage is attached to the rest of the home by a door that leads into a hallway. On the right of the hallway and on the street's side is a room with a display of urns and memorial plaques and all the different kinds of caskets.

And on the other side of the hallway are a supply room and then a small flower room — mainly just a bunch of shelves — where delivery people from the various floral shops can drop off arrangements and wreaths through an outside door off the back parking lot. The flower room's inside door off the hallway is kept locked so nobody can gain entrance from the back lot even when the outside door is unlocked during office hours.

If you go farther down the hallway, you come to the front entrance, a main office and the two viewing rooms — one big and one small. And like I said earlier, the prep room — or embalming room if that sounds any better — a kitchen and a few more offices are upstairs.

I guess it's your typical funeral home — even though the only other one I was in was when my real dad died. And I wasn't exactly doing a lot of observing on that day. I do remember a big bowl of mints on a table out in the hallway and I ate about a hundred of them.

I reminded Kelly again that I wasn't doing any guided tours. I was sort of ashamed of myself that we were inside anyway. The Dixon brothers have been pretty good to me but I've heard a few of their stories about how they would take their friends into the funeral home when their dad owned it.

They told how one of their friends peed his pants when they took him into the casket room in the dark and pretended that there were bodies in all of them. Then another buddy popped out of one to scare the poor guy. They thought that was great fun. I'm not sure they would laugh if I was caught doing the same thing, though.

I left the lights off but there was enough to see in the casket room because of the nearest street light shining through the windows. It was pretty eerie, though, even for me. Kelly and Wheat were still out in the hallway. Wheat was looking a little like a dog that didn't want to go any further on its walk with Kelly trying to coax her on.

"There aren't any bodies in here," I said.

"You better be right, buster," she said.

"Maybe some ashes in urns from the dearly departed but ashes don't make very good ghosts."

"Come on, Spank. She's scared enough as it is," Kelly said.

"I'm just kidding," I said. "There are urns but they're all empty, just like the coffins. Come on, Wheat. Face your fears. You're always saying that to me about wrestling stuff."

She moved forward. It was going to be hard for me not to mention to her that I knew there was a container over in the storage room of a woman's ashes. Her husband wanted them to be saved until he died, too, so his ashes could be mixed with hers. Maybe that's romantic to some people, but I'm not seeing it right now.

I also had peeked down the hallway and into the larger visitation room and saw there was indeed a body — it looked like an elderly woman — in a casket. So they must have had a viewing earlier in the day and that she was all ready for her funeral tomorrow morning. I stayed still about that.

Wheat and Kelly, kind of locked together, came through the door to the casket room. Kelly suddenly looked as uncomfortable as Wheat

"Just empty caskets," I said, not daring to mention the elderly woman down the way. "No corpses, no vampires, no mummies."

Caskets are actually kind of cool, especially the ones made out of fine wood. I know this sounds a little weird for a 15-year-old kid to be saying but to me, they would look like fancy soap box derby racers if they had wheels. I can hear it now: "Drivers, start your coffins." I think a famous sports writer once said that about the Indianapolis 500 and he wasn't trying to be funny. Yeah, I know. Creepy.

"You still want to get in one?" I asked Kelly.

He didn't answer.

"Come on, man," I said. "I'm taking a big chance bringing you in here. You wanted to come. Am I going to have to double-dog dare you now?"

"Okay, okay," he said. "I can do this. But you're doing it, too, remember?"

I did. I opened the top of the oaken one that was sitting on a stand. Kelly, without saying a word, hopped right in. It was a pretty amazing athletic move.

"Hey, I high jumped 5-foot-11 in junior high," he said when both Wheat sort of went "Woooo!" together.

I closed the bottom half and there Kelly was, lying like Snow White before the big kiss. I didn't mention that. I was afraid that Wheat would want to play the role of Princess Charming and kiss this froggy.

"This is pretty comfortable," Kelly said, doing a pretend yawn like he was going to fall asleep.

"Now your turn, Spank," Wheat said.

I wasn't going to be able to flop in there like Kelly so I walked across the hall to the storage room to get a little two-step ladder. As I grabbed it, I thought I heard something near the outside door to the flower room.

That gave me the heebie-jeebies. I sneaked over to the window and peeked through the blinds. I felt my heartbeat in my throat — Hummingbird Heart paying me a visit again. Uh-oh. I spied the rusty old car out in the parking lot that Wheat and I saw when we were shoveling the snow a few days earlier. And then I saw a couple of guys — one little and one big — trying to break in the flower room's outside door.

I froze, but only for a moment because somebody put a hand on my back. I could have jumped high enough to completely clear a casket.

"What's that noise?" Wheat whispered.

"Shhhh. A couple of guys are trying to break in and I think it might be the One-Booted Man and his sidekick," I whispered back. "Look at that car."

"What do we do?" Wheat said as she grabbed my arm really, really hard.

"Hide," I said.

"This would be one time I wish we would always carry our cell phone around," Wheat said. "I left it back on my desk."

"Just great," I thought.

We hustled back into the casket room and I quickly told Kelly what was going on and to call 911 on his cell phone.

"Shoot!" he moaned. "I'm out of power. So should we confront them?"

"If it's who I think it is, I figure one could have some kind of weapon," I said. "Let's keep out of their sight. If it looks like they're going to do something really bad, we'll surprise them. I'll sneak down to the office and call 911 and then Dad while you guys hide in the caskets."

- 142 -

"Not me," she gasped.

"Yes, you," I hissed. "Best place to hide. I'll stick something under the lid so you're not completely closed in. It's hard to see in here anyway."

"Just great," she moaned.

Then she climbed up the little two-step ladder and got in the mahogany one. I don't think she wanted to look too scared in front of Kelly but I could tell she was really agitated. I stuck a photo album between the lid and the top half of the casket so there was a two-inch gap. I then went over and closed the lid over Kelly.

As I headed down the hallway, I heard the inside door to the flower room being jimmied. Maybe this wasn't such a great plan. I dove into the office just as I heard the inside flower room door give way. I hid under the desk.

"You go into the room over there with the caskets and see if there's anything worth taking," I heard the guy with the raspy voice say. "I'm going to check out the old lady they got in here. Her step-nephew said she would probably be buried in some of her expensive jewelry. He said she was a real scrooge."

"That's sick," said his little accomplice.

I agreed with him. I didn't think I could let that happen. I reached up for the phone and dialed 911.

But at that very moment, I heard a bang from the casket room and Wheat gasp, "I can't breathe!"

I dropped the phone and headed that way. Right behind me, I heard the One-Booted Man coming, apparently with a complete set of boots on. For some reason, I wondered if he had to go out and buy a whole other pair.

As I raced through the door, I scanned the room quickly and saw that Wheat had managed to climb out of her casket and Kelly had thrown open the top of his and was trying to get out when the little guy slammed it down on his head. That didn't sound so good.

"There are people in these caskets!" the little guy almost shrieked as I raced over and picked up an urn and threw it at him.

t missed but while he was ducking, Wheat took him down just like he was Thirsty Thurston.

And then I saw stars as the One-Booted Man hit me with something that careened off my shoulder and into the side of my head. Because I was a moving target, I don't think he got off the perfect blow he was intending.

But I went down anyway and was pretty stunned. I'm not sure what happened next but I heard a shriek that could have just about awakened the elderly lady out in the viewing room.

For a moment, I thought it was Wheat although I never had heard her scream in my life.

Then I heard the little guy cry out, "I think she broke my shoulder."

I pulled myself into a sitting position and saw the little guy slinking toward the door, his right arm hanging at his side. I could see through the light in the window that Wheat was now up and facing the One-Booted Man.

"Well, I guess you picked on somebody your own size but now you got me," he said to Wheat.

He was patting something in his hand just like he had after I tried to tackle him last week in the neighborhood. I recognized now that it was a tire iron.

I charged him from behind and when I hit him, I realized that he was almost as huge as Big Jim. He didn't go all the way down but he stumbled forward and Wheat was able to knee him in the face, knocking something out of his mouth. He sounded like a wounded grizzly bear and we all know they can be dangerous.

He was, too. He swung the tire iron at Wheat — who had let herself get too close to him — and caught her on the side of her face. She went down like a rock in water. I started to go to her but the One-Booted Man, blood dripping out of his mouth, swung the tire iron at me. I was able to jump out of the way, but barely.

I wanted to help Wheat but I figured that ending up beside her in the same situation wasn't going to be good for either of us. There was only one way to save the day: Run. As I did, I scooped up what had fallen out of One-Booted's mouth and saw that it was dentures.

He was on my heels again. I headed for the stairs to the second floor and he lunged at me when I was about four steps up. He caught me by my foot. Wouldn't you know it, my tennis shoe came off.

"Now, we're even!" I yelled back as I pulled away.

"You think so, you little ..." he said.

Yeah, well, again I'm not going to tell you what he called me. "I know you now. You're the little punk who stole my boot. I thought I recognized you when I saw you shoveling snow the other day. Where's your cop friend when you need him? And give me back my teeth."

Maybe I should have. But I figured if he was chasing me, he was going the opposite direction of Wheat. And the longer I kept him after me, the better chance of somebody coming to our rescue. But if I just gave him his teeth back, maybe he would leave and nobody else — mainly me — would get hurt.

Oh, well. I had made my decision. And I think his lunging at me and his talking slowed him down because I seemed to get a bit of a lead rushing the rest of the way up the stairs. There was only one light on up on the second floor, too, and I knew where the switch was — a little behind the refrigerator in the kitchen where nobody could find it unless they already knew about it. I had just enough of a lead for me to flip it off before he could see what I had done. Now it was pitch black.

I heard One Boot bang into the door frame to the kitchen and then apparently stop. I creeped down the two little steps to the prep room and one of them gave a little creak.

"If you want to play hide-and-seek, that's what we'll do," he said and he came closer.

He then stumbled down the two steps. He said a few more bad words.

I could hear him feeling for a switch but the only lights in the prep room are the hanging ones over the work areas with chains to pull. He was coming across the room — about 10 feet away from me. But I had a plan, actually a plan I had just thought of when I realized I was right in front of the open elevator shaft.

"I may not see you but I smell you, you little pansy," he said, apparently getting a whiff of the Midnight Breeze that was still permeating off me. "A little twerp shouldn't smell so sweet. Let me have my teeth and I'll leave you alone."

He came closer, now about five feet away and I could hear him breathing.

I got into a wrestler's stance and then whispered, "Bite me, Tooth Decay."

He rushed in my direction just as I did a pancake move onto the floor. He stumbled over my body and went tripping into the elevator shaft — I figured a little like Gollum going into the fire on Mount Doom.

He yelled something I couldn't understand and then I heard him hit the bottom. I rushed over and pulled the cord on one of the hanging lights and then looked down the shaft. The platform was all the way into the basement and he was lying there in a grotesque pose. He was also groaning. It didn't look like he was going anywhere soon except on a gurney.

I went speeding downstairs while flipping on lights as I went and found Wheat still on the floor. She was breathing okay and moaning a little to herself. I started to head for the office to call for an ambulance but then I saw the red-and-blue lights of a squad car heading into the parking lot. I guess my 911 call had gone through and they were able to track our location.

And then I heard Kelly.

"Can anybody let me out?"

The little guy had apparently pulled the lock on the casket after he had slammed its top down on Kelly's head. I opened it and Kelly had a knot on his forehead about the size of a golf ball. But he seemed okay.

He got out slowly and I told him to stay with Wheat while I opened the garage door for the police officers. A couple of them came hustling in and I took them to the basement steps and told them about One Boot.

By the time I got back to Wheat and Kelly, he was starting to give her what looked like artificial respiration.

"She doesn't need that, you dunce."

"How do you know?" Wheat said weakly.

Kelly stopped. "You okay?" he asked her.

"My face feels like it's broken but a few more of what you were doing might help."

Kelly leaned down and gave her what looked more like a kiss rather than any kind of help in breathing. I stood there for a second and then figured that three was a crowd. I went out into the hall just as Dad came rushing in through the garage. In a few minutes, there were a couple more squad cars, two ambulances and a lot of neighbors out on the sidewalk.

CHAPTER 20

When the dust finally settled, it was determined that the One Booted Man — real name Dex Glass — had two broken legs, three broken ribs and a concussion from his fall and a swollen mouth minus his dentures. His accomplice — Jerry Simpleman, an appropriate name, I thought — had a torn ligament in his shoulder.

Wheat had a broken cheekbone and might need surgery when the swelling went down. Kelly had his knot, quickly turning black and blue like some kind of geode we studied in freshman science. And I had a little bit of the shakes that I was trying hard to hide from everyone.

Glass and Simpleman were both in custody with Glass also in the hospital. Both were being linked to several other break-ins in our part of town. Glass had a criminal record that included assault with a deadly weapon. Simpleman was more of a shoplifter type. The police had picked him up a few blocks from the funeral home and he was claiming that he had been a victim of an assault.

It was just as well that there were a half a dozen other cops at the funeral home because Dad was definitely not showing any sympathy for Glass's injury. He might have thrown him down the elevator shaft again if his law enforcement buddies hadn't kept him away from Glass as the EMTs carted him off.

I was considered a bit of a hero even if all I really did was drop to the floor and trip the guy — and steal his teeth, too. The Dixon brothers were very grateful we stopped a burglary and the possible tampering with a body. Because of that, they didn't seem too upset that we were climbing into their caskets. I'm not sure the cops gave them the whole story but I figured it reminded them of their own shenanigans when they were younger.

Mom and Dad weren't as understanding. They said if I didn't have the conference meet coming up, I would probably be grounded immediately for taking Wheat and Kelly into the funeral home.

I felt guilty that it was my decision that got Wheat hurt and I felt tears run down my cheeks for the second time in a day. Wheat had been taken to the hospital by ambulance, too, but came home later in the evening. She had been given some strong pain medicine and seemed a little loopy, but she understood she wasn't going to be wrestling in the conference meet.

Mom and Dad sort of tucked us into bed that night. They hadn't done that in a long time. They treated me almost as tenderly as they did Wheat even though I knew there would be a reckoning at some point.

I think I saw a tear in Dad's eye as he gave me a kiss on the forehead. Mom asked Wheat to lean her head down the side of her top bunk so she could do the same.

At that point, I wailed, "I'm sorry!"

Nobody said anything for a moment until I heard the weak voice of Wheat above me.

"Knock it off, Spank. Kelly talked you into taking us in there and I wasn't exactly dragged in. You took care of that big guy with your sneakiness."

"And you took care of the little guy," I sniffled.

"Yeah," Wheat almost whispered. "That was kind of fun."

Dad laughed at that and I think Mom even smiled a little. At that point, they said they had just gotten home before all the commotion after making an offer on the house out in the country. They said they would talk about that later with us.

Then they told us to get some sleep. That was pretty hard to do. I heard Wheat whimpering a little from time to time and any time I fell off to sleep, it seemed I dreamed about the One Booted Man chasing us. At one point, he had werewolf teeth and I must have let out a noise.

Then I heard Wheat say, "I'm coming down."

I moved over against the wall and she climbed into bed beside me.

"I just don't want to be up there alone after all that has happened. And I'm having some Spank-like dreams — or nightmares."

We laid side by side and it was a comforting feeling. I had to say it again, though.

"I'm so sorry, Wheat."

"I know you are," she said. "But it will be all right. We did good tonight even though we shouldn't have been doing what we were doing. And don't worry about me and the wrestling. I'm a sophomore. I'll have other chances to win the conference — and maybe the state."

"I don't think I can wrestle if you don't," I told her.

"Don't go there, Spank. You wrestle for both of us. You do your best. When the going gets tough …"

"Yeah, I know … the tough get going."

"Now go to sleep."

And so I did. I think she did, too. Before I knew it, it was morning and Wheat was snoring. The left side of her face was swollen but she still looked sort of like an angel to me.

I carefully climbed over her and went down for breakfast.

———

Mom and Dad let Wheat sleep in. She wasn't going to school anyway. She had an appointment with a surgeon.

"Ta-da," Lake kept saying when she didn't join the family for breakfast.

"She still has an ouchie," Mom finally said.

Of course, Lake repeated "Ouchie." We're giving that kid quite an early vocabulary.

I wish I could have stayed home from school, too, because I was the one who was going to have to explain to everyone what happened

Big Jim and Sally already knew, though.

"Kelly called me last night and told me all about it," Sally said. "It sounds like you saved the day, Sir William. I'm impressed. Even Kelly seemed impressed."

Her brother wasn't as impressed, though.

"How are we going to win the conference if Wheat isn't going to be able to wrestle?" he asked.

I didn't know what to tell him.

"I should have warned you more," Big Jim added. "You hang around Kelly Carson and see what happens."

"You just don't like him because we painted your face pink and purple when you fell asleep that Easter and you were supposed to be helping us with the Easter eggs," Sally said.

We pulled into the parking lot and Big Jim stormed off. Sally just sat in the front seat. I got out and waited. She just kept sitting. I stood there for a while and then opened her door to see if she was okay.

"Thank you, kind sir," she said as she climbed out. "I know you wanted to do that."

I figured I would keep it to myself that I opened her door more out of curiosity than courtesy. She gave me a sly grin and I wondered which Sally I was going to get — and if she was going to plant one on me again.

"Hey, Spank, Kelly told me he might take your sister to the dance if she felt up to it. She apparently can't wrestle Saturday, right?"

I nodded, wondering where this was going.

"Well, why don't we double with them since you're apparently a free man now that Laurie Middlebrook's soldier boy is back in town?"

I gulped but thought I might give it to her a little.

"Well, there is a chance I might be in the championship round of the conference meet," I said.

"Well, I'll come and watch you and we can go from there," she said.

"One condition," I said.

"What's that?" she laughed. "A condition, Little Man?"

"What did I tell you about calling me Little Man?" I huffed.

"Oh, sorry, Sir William. And what would Your Worthiness's one condition be?"

"If you wear that yellow dress that you had on at dance class on Monday."

"You liked me in that dress?"

"Pretty much."

"That old thing? Well, I was thinking of something else but I can see what I can do. I do like that yellow dress, too. I'll see if I have the right accessories to go along with it."

What did that mean, I wondered.

She actually grabbed my hand as we walked into the school.

"Saturday is going to be a big day. You think my brother has a chance of winning his weight?"

The way my mind was working, I had almost forgotten she had a brother … or mother … or an orneriness when dealing with me just a few days ago. My mind was trying to take everything in that had happened to me in the last half day.

"Earth to Spank, earth to Spank," Sally said.

"Yeah," I said.

"Yeah, what?"

"Yeah, I'll go with you."

"I thought we already established that. My brother. What about him?"

"What about him?" I repeated. "You want him to go, too?"

"Never mind. Call me tonight."

"Call you what? Ohhh, call you on the phone."

"Spank, are you sure your sister and Kelly were the only ones who got conked last night?" she asked as she started to head the other way down the hall.

I just smiled as I once again watched her glide down the hallway. I had to wonder if maybe I could someday find just a sort-of-cute but sweet girl who made me feel like I didn't have to be constantly living up to my legend.

My situation made me think of a couple of other homophones — prey and pray. I felt like I was the former and needed to do the latter. How about I say I'm on a homophone high — ha, ha — just so I can use a little more alliteration? I'm a real word warrior. Get it?

CHAPTER 21

The news quickly spread in school about what had happened at the funeral home. I guess the knot on Kelly's noggin was like a press release. A few of our teammates came up to me and commiserated about Wheat. A couple of guys kidded me about how tough I was.

Both the Brayton brothers, Billy and Bobby, said nice things to me. Bobby's girlfriend, Ellie Robistelli, even gave me a thumbs-up out in the hallway and called out, "Way to go, tiger." She may make my Top 5 list pretty soon.

I guess the news hadn't spread into Laurie Middlebrook's circle of friends, though. She smiled at me when I came into English class and then asked me if I was liking a couple of Robert Frost poems we were supposed to be studying.

I said I did, especially the one about good fences making good neighbors, although I couldn't think of the name of the poem. She couldn't either, and we both sat there trying to think of it, allowing any awkwardness to pass while we waited for the bell to ring.

I was glad I didn't have to talk to her about the One Booted Man and Wheat's injury and Kelly Carson's noggin. I told Bobby Taylor not to bring it up around her but that wasn't really necessary. Other than Wheat, I don't think Bobby has talked to a girl since grade school.

Of course, Coach Mathews already knew about Wheat. Dad had called him in the morning. When I got to the wrestling room after school, he waved me into his office.

"Tough about your sister," he said. "She would have won the conference and then been one of the top seeds for the state tournament. I'm glad she's just a sophomore"

I agreed. Then he asked me how much I weighed.

"I was almost up to 115 this morning and that was before breakfast," I said.

"Can you lose enough to take your sister's spot at 113 tomorrow?" he asked.

"Maybe," I said, holding back the groan.

"Well, you obviously would have a better chance of advancing at the lower weight and I think Benny is back in good enough shape that he could maybe win a match tomorrow at 120. Don't repeat this, but if I wrestled the Torso at 113 against a top-notch wrestler, they might arrest me for child abuse. The poor kid is just not a varsity wrestler."

I agreed but didn't say so. I was thinking more about the nice meal I was going to be missing tonight.

"I've lost three or four pounds before," I said. "I can do it."

Coach Mathews smiled.

"I think that will give us a better chance of winning the meet and maybe a chance for you to take the 113 title. You're on a bit of a roll anyway. Some sort of hero last night. Just curious. Do you think your wrestling background helped?"

I said it did. I knew that would make Coach happy. And I guess I did react quickly and knew how to avoid that charging moose. Maybe I kept my cool, too. I don't know. I would have to think a little more on how much my wrestling might have helped me handle the situation. I do know the time I was most scared was after everything was over and I relived how it had turned out.

"You good with all this, Spank?" Coach Mathews said. "You look like you're somewhere else. I know you've had a crazy day or two and it has to be upsetting about Wheat. If you want to go ahead and stay at 120, we can do that. I know you have some work ahead of you if you are going to lose the weight."

"I'll be good at 113," I assured him.

"Great," he said. "Now round up the rest of the guys for a quick meeting and then everybody can do what they need to do."

The meeting was a bit somber because of the news about Wheat — most knew the story anyway — and then Coach went over our lineup and surprised Benny that he was going to get back his 120 spot. He looked happy.

The conference meet was going to be at Penn High School with the morning session starting at 9. I would have to win two matches in the morning to advance to the semifinals in the afternoon and then win that to get into the evening finals.

After Coach got done talking, we all got into a circle and put our hands together. Dion Borden told how we were going to whump on Penn and Mishawaka and then Big Jim, as emotional as I have seen him, said we were going win the meet for Wheat.

Then the chanting started.

"Win for Wheat! Win for Wheat!"

Guys started chest bumping each other and Benny came over and gave me a big hug.

"Thanks, Spank," he said. "I'm so happy I'm getting the chance."

Then Tommy the Torso hugged me, too. He was as happy as Benny because he wasn't going to have to fill in at 113.

While most of the guys headed home, I put on a sweat suit and started running laps around the gym. I figured I could take the weight off if I ran for an hour. Sherman Nelson, our 182-pounder, was running, too.

We call him Tank — Sherman Tank, get it? He's a pretty good football lineman but just an average wrestler. This Tank is known to run out of gas. He is heavy to the metal in the first period but if an opponent can avoid getting pinned during that time, he can usually outlast the Tanker. Yeah, he tanks about halfway through the second period. Of all our nicknames, his might be the most appropriate — in more ways than one.

I didn't think a bunch of running was going to help him the day before the conference. He didn't usually have weight to lose.

"You over, Tank?" I asked as I passed him on a lap.

"I'm pretty much right on weight," he said. "But my little sister turned 13 today and I want to have some of her birthday cake. I figure if I lose a couple of pounds running, I can eat a couple of pieces."

"So you want to have your cake and eat it, too," I said as I stayed beside him for several slow strides.

"What does that mean?" he asked.

"I don't really know," I admitted. "My granddad has always said that. I think it might mean that…"

"Beat it, Spank," he said. "I don't care what it means and I don't need to be having any more conversations while I'm trying to work up a sweat. You little guys always tick me off with how easily you can run."

I scooted along. I should have probably told him that I didn't think the cake was going to be good for him right before the meet.

I ran for almost an hour. The Tank made it for about 20 minutes. I wasn't sure that was going to allow him a second piece of cake. But he still could have one and eat one, I thought, and still wondered what that stupid expression meant.

Sweat was pouring off me when I went back to the locker room. I stripped down to my tighty whities — I gave up my Spiderman undies when I started high school — and got on the scales. I was just a little under 114 and so I felt pretty good. I could lose another pound before morning easy enough. I called Dad on our cell phone and he said he could pick me up.

Maddie Hamilton came in to pick up towels and looked embarrassed that I was sitting there without a shirt on and with my three tiny chest hairs sticking straight out.

"Oh, sorry, Spank," she said. "I thought everyone was gone."

"It's just me and Bobby Magee," I said.

It's a line from an old song that I've heard my Grandma Kate sometimes sing. Maddie apparently hadn't heard it.

"Is he a new kid?" she asked.

I laughed.

"No, no, that's from a song," I said. "It's just me."

She looked like she was turning red and I guess I noticed — maybe for the first time — that she was kind of cute. Long blonde hair, pretty teeth and dimples. I like dimples. She might be in the 145-pound class and a couple of inches taller than me but so what? I wasn't planning on wrestling her. And I'm beginning to think that size doesn't have to be such a big deal — unless you have to lose a couple of pounds for a meet.

"Well, good luck, Spank," she said as she headed quickly for the door with a pile of dirty towels. "You've always been one of my favorite wrestlers."

Geez, I am barely average, I thought. What's with that girl? I wanted to ask her a couple of questions but Mr. Gunderson, the sports facilities' custodian, was the only one around when I came out of the locker room. He can't hear worth a darn so it's hard to talk with him. So I just waved when I went by as he pushed a broom across the floor.

"You the last one?" he yelled.

"Yes, sir," I yelled back.

"You wrestling tomorrow?"

I yelled out another, "Yes, sir."

"Then good luck and don't call me sir," he yelled, upping the decibels even more. "I was a gunnery sergeant, not an officer. We didn't have much use for them around the artillery."

"Is that what affected your hearing, Mr. Gunderson," I almost screeched.

"What are you hearing?" he shouted back, looking like he was expecting some gossip from me.

"I gotta go," I replied and gave him a wave.

I was going to lose my voice if I hung around any longer. To be honest, I think a conversation with Mr. Gunderson would tire me out more than a run.

Dad was waiting in his squad car outside the gym and said that Wheat got a pretty good prognosis from the doctor. She might be able to avoid any kind of plastic surgery but that she would definitely not be wrestling for a while.

He said that Simpleman sang like a stool pigeon about the various houses and cars that he and Glass — the One Booted Man — had hit. Simpleman even mentioned the names of a couple of fences they used to get rid of the stuff. So it was a good day for the good guys.

"We might get the house," Dad said as he turned onto our street. "We're just waiting to see if the owners will accept our offer. You've got enough to worry about right now and so we can talk about it later."

"That's good, I said and meant it. My mind was already pretty close to overload.

At home, I found Wheat sitting on the couch with Lake on her lap. "Ta-da, ouchie," Lake said as he pointed up to Wheat's black and blue cheek.

"You hanging in there?" I asked.

"Sore, but okay," she said. "What about you?"

"Okay, but I'm going to be masquerading as you tomorrow — a 113-pound terror."

"I'd smile if it wouldn't hurt. You have a good chance of advancing pretty far."

We talked a little more and I yelled out to the kitchen to mom that I was just going to have a bowl of chicken broth for dinner and maybe some Jell-O.

She came into the dining room and looked disappointed. "I made a big dish of lasagna — mainly for you and your carbo-loading."

"I'll eat it for leftovers all next week," I told her and explained my weight class change.

"Okay," she said. "I'll warm up the soup for you."

Being the mom of a wrestler isn't always easy, I know, and I felt a little bad for her. She's a great cook. Not a neat one — the kitchen sometimes looks like a disaster after she's done preparing a meal but she could probably be a chef if she wanted to in my opinion. That's as long as there was someone else to clean up after her. The rest of her house would pass any white-glove treatment but the kitchen sometimes lags behind.

Wheat and I talked about the wrestling meeting and I told her how the guys had chanted her name. I could tell she was touched even if she tried not to show it. Lake waddled off to the kitchen and Wheat told me she was at least going to try to go to the winter formal for a little while with Kelly — maybe for some punch and a couple of slow dances.

"Unless you're in the finals, of course," she said.

"At 120, it was probably going to be a pretty quick meet for me," I said. "Maybe I can win the morning matches at 113, but there are too many good guys for me to make the finals."

Then I changed the subject.

"You and Kelly? Are Mom and Dad okay with that?"

"They're okay with it. I knew they would be fine. It's you who I worry about."

I wasn't sure what to say. Wheat is the most important person in my life right now and I hoped that was how she felt about me, too. A boyfriend could complicate that closeness we have. And Kelly Carson of all people. He's probably a better guy than I thought he was a few days ago but he still was going to be one of those pretty boys all his born days. Then again, maybe he'll lose all his hair by the time he's 25.

"I'm okay with it, too," I finally said.

"I hear you may be keeping an eye on me anyway," she said.

"Kelly told me this afternoon that you and Sally may be doubling with us. That is, if you aren't in the finals tomorrow. Wow, Spank. A cheerleader … a junior … a dancing queen … and a crazy woman. All rolled into one."

I hadn't forgotten about Sally. But I had tried to push her out of my mind for a while, which might be like forgetting how to breathe.

"I hear there's a chance we might be moving to that house," Wheat added. "What are you thinking?"

"I'll be a little sad if it happens, but we'll get our own rooms," I answered.

She nodded. So did I. And we let it go. Maybe we were thinking the same thing, if I could figure out exactly what I was thinking.

I went off to weigh myself and then ate my meager dinner. Lake decided he wanted Jell-O, too. Then I got a call on our house phone from a newspaper reporter. She was doing a story on the police catching the guys who had been breaking into homes and cars and heard that I had played a part in it.

I didn't know what to say since we should have never been in the funeral home in the first place.

I hemmed and hawed a little and then finally mumbled, "I really didn't do much."

But then she said, "Todd Dixon said you were a hero, that you were doing some work for them at the funeral home and apparently out-foxed the burglars."

Well if Todd Dixon said it …

"I guess I tricked a guy into falling down an elevator shaft," I said. "Actually, he sort of tripped over me in the dark."

"One of the police officers told me you and your sister are wrestlers," she continued. "Did that help in any way?"

She sounded like Coach Mathews.

"I'm trying to weigh 113 pounds for tomorrow's conference meet," I answered. "That guy must have weighed around 240, I'm guessing. I think track would have helped me a lot more than wrestling."

She laughed at that. Then she asked about Wheat and some other things about what I do at the funeral home and if I wanted to be a cop like Dad. She also heard that we had a confrontation with the burglars on one of our morning runs.

"Yeah, I tackled the big guy's boot," I said and explained. "I called him the One-Booted Man but he had two boots on last night."

She liked my nickname for him and wished me good luck the rest of the wrestling season. She said there would be a story in the paper tomorrow.

I figured I was going to have to move to a bigger city. I was getting too well-known around our town — ha, ha.

I was about to put on a sweat suit and jog up and down our basement steps for a half hour when Wheat came into our room with our cell.

"Somebody on the phone asking for Sir William," she said, rather sarcastically.

"That would be me," I said.

Wheat just shook her head and left.

"You were going to call me, weren't you, Sir William?" Sally said. "Other late offers to take me to the dance are rolling in and so I wanted to make sure you and I are still going to be out in the limelight together."

"Like I said, only if you wear that yellow dress," I said.

"Oh, the things I do for you."

Hard as I tried, I couldn't think of anything that she had ever done for me but give me a life-changing kiss.

Finally, Sally said, "Are you still there, Sir William?

"Yes."

"Usually, boys want to talk to me a little longer when they call me."

"You called me," I pointed out.

"That I did. So I'll see you at the wrestling meet tomorrow and we can make our plans. I assume your sister and Kelly are going. If not, you're going to have to ride me there on your bicycle's handlebars since I flunked my first try at passing my driver's test."

"What happened?" I had to ask.

"Oh, the stupid instructor said I bumped a car behind us when I was parallel parking. I don't think I've ever seen my mom parallel park in her life but I'm not driving yet because I barely brushed another car while doing an otherwise perfect maneuver. The way the instructor acted, it was as if it was his car I tapped."

"That's too bad," I said, sort of relieved that I wasn't going to be alone in a car with Sally.

I don't think I have enough testosterone — is that the right word? — just yet for that kind of closeness with a girl like Sally. Maybe I wouldn't feel that same way with Laurie Middlebrook. Then again, maybe I would.

"What are you doing right now, Sir William?" she continued.

"Trying to lose a couple of pounds."

"Aren't we all?" she said before hanging up.

I looked down at my hand that had been holding the phone and sweat was dripping off of it. Maybe if I had talked with Sally another five minutes or so, I wouldn't have to run the basement steps.

CHAPTER 22

I got up at 5:30 the next morning after a restless night. Lots of crazy dreams. The one I remember most was with me in the passenger seat while Sally was driving a Hummer. She slammed on the brakes and a big pile of my mom's lasagna that I was eating flew all over my pants. I need to start having better dreams.

I needed to be at the school at 7 for the bus ride over to Penn High School. Weigh-ins would be at 8 and the meet would start at 9.

I didn't know what worried me most — wrestling in the conference meet or going to the winter formal with Sally Guffie. I didn't bother to wake up Wheat, who was snoring a little again on the top bunk. I know she will deny that she's ever snored. Maybe I need to record her some time before we end up in our separate bedrooms

I went into the bathroom and weighed myself. I was a just a little over 113. I went down and drank part of one of Wheat's Diet Cokes from the fridge. I know that sounds like I am defeating the purpose of losing weight by drinking something. But the caffeine in a Coke, especially in the morning, turns me into a fire hose.

Dad was alone at the kitchen table. He pushed the paper over to me. I couldn't believe it? There was my school picture with a story about the foiled burglary under a Page 3 headline that read: "Prep Wrestler Gives Bandit the Boot."

"Well, there's your 15 minutes of fame, Spank," he said. "Do you think that you can get a few minutes more later today?"

I just smiled. I decided not to read the story and told Dad so. I had enough on my plate — which, I've told you before, is not a very good saying for a guy who was going to eat a little leftover orange Jell-O for breakfast.

"I think the writer made the story sound a little more amusing than it needed to be," he continued. "It almost reads like Jack and the Beanstalk. The guy was dangerous and he hurt your sister. But the writer, Emily Davis, made you look pretty good in it. It will probably get you more attention than you want."

All I wanted was to do well in the conference, dance with Sally at the winter formal while trying to keep my nose clear of her cleavage (that might be my best alliteration of all) and try to be in one piece at the end of the night. Okay, and maybe another major kiss. Then I was thinking of shaving off my peach fuzz again so nobody would recognize me — ha, ha — and hiding out in the non-fiction section of the school library for a few weeks. That would be good.

Dad must have been reading my mind.

"I know it's a big day, Spank. Just do your best. That's all you can do. Do your best. And, really, nothing else matters."

"Any suggestions about taking Sally Guffie to the dance?" I asked.

"You're on your own there, bud," he said with a chuckle. "That might be your toughest match-up of the day."

"Thanks for the advice," I said.

He reached over and patted my shoulder.

"Ah, to be 18 years old again," he said.

"I'm 15," I replied.

"Well, I never ran into a girl like Sally Guffie until I was 18," he laughed.

"Daaad!" I whined and then gave him a curious look.

"Some other time," he said. "Go get ready. Just remember that girls — even the tough ones like Wheat and this Sally — are always to be treated with the utmost respect. That's what makes a man a man."

I nodded and headed off to the bathroom to do my business. When I was finished and stripped down to my birthday suit, I was almost exactly 113 pounds — and our scales are pretty darn accurate.

Mom and Lake were up by that time. Mom gave me a hug and Lake looked at me like I was some sort of rock star. I think he is getting to like me almost as much as he does Wheat. If I get beat really bad in the conference, I just hope his memory doesn't go back this far when he's older.

Wheat was still sleeping and that was probably a good thing. I felt I had enough weight on my shoulders without including her 113 pounds. I realized again how terrible I felt that she wasn't going to be wrestling. I was glad she wasn't going to see me head out the door to take her place.

I grabbed an apple, banana, granola bar and my jar of honey that I would snack on over the course of the day after I made weight. I wondered how I would be when I walked back into our house 16 or so hours from now. At least I hoped I was still walking.

"Let's roll," I said to Dad and we were out the door before Mom could give me one of her corny pep talks or before Wheat came down the stairs.

When I walked into the locker room, everybody there gave me a standing ovation and Jack Winkler, our 152-pounder, held up the article in the newspaper with my face in it. "Spanky, Spanky, Spanky," they cheered. Locker room chants usually aren't very original.

Then Thirsty walked in like he was bursting at the seams and announced excitedly, "I finally got up to 100 pounds!"

Everybody cheered again and started chanting, "Thirsty, Thirsty, Thirsty."

Then getting into the spirit of things, Dion Borden spewed out something about his … oh, I can't tell you. It wasn't very nice but it was kind of funny. So we yelled, "Dion, Dion, Dion."

Then Big Jim said, "Let's not forget about Wheat."

And so the team all started yelling out her name again.

At that point, Coach Mathews joined us and said it didn't look like we needed a pep talk. But he gave us one anyway. It was pretty good. He can sometimes go all Knute Rockne on us but I guess he figured we were already pretty pumped up. So he talked normally — as normally as a coach can before a big event — and told us about his conference meet during his junior year. He won, Clay won. "Besides my wedding day and the birth of my two kids, it was maybe the best day of my life," he said.

Yikes! I didn't think I was old enough to have those kind of lasting memories yet. But I guess it made me happy that Coach Mathews still remembered what it felt like to be a high school kid. He's got to be close to 35.

After we got in our uniforms, we boarded the school bus. Mr. Maroney is usually our driver. He never says a word to us except "Shut up!" when we come to a railroad crossing even if we aren't hardly saying anything. We could be the New York Yankees and he would probably still be yelling "Shut up!" and scowling at us.

Once, Coach Mathews said something to Mr. Maroney about his yelling. But then Mr. Maroney replied, "Weren't you the kid who threw the bananas out the window a few years back and got me pulled over by a cop?"

Coach Mathews didn't say anything else. I guess maybe he had been that kid.

Our bus trips are never boring. Some guys will spit into a cup to lose another few ounces if they are a little over weight. I've never had to do that and really don't want to sit beside someone who is doing it. The Sherman Tank was known to be a little reckless with his aim before he went up a weight.

So I sat down beside Big Jim because at heavyweight, he doesn't have to worry about weight. I've seen him eat a Big Mac and fries on a bus trip over to a meet. That made a lot of guys mad, especially the ones who had had to cut weight. But who is going to tell Big Jim to stop eating?

"You and my sister, huh," he said. "Watch yourself Spank. You might want to wear your headgear to the dance just in case. She may come out of the spell that our grandma cast on her at any time."

Maddie Hamilton was sitting behind us all alone and looking uncomfortable. She usually sits with Wheat on the bus rides to meets. I always wanted to ask her why a nice girl like her wanted to be a wrestling manager but I figured I didn't need to hear some long story right now.

I just gave her a nod and she smiled back. That felt good.

CHAPTER 23

Everybody made weight after we got there. I was at 112 and three-quarters after a trip to the rest room. Thirsty made sure we all broke ranks in our lineup behind the scales to see that he actually had made it to 100.

Not long after the weigh-in and during the first meet of the day, a kid from Elkhart had no trouble taking the bigger-but-no-better Thirsty down. He was pinned in about a half minute.

"Maybe if he had gained about 50 pounds he could have won," Benny Goodchild whispered to me.

We were watching from the other side of the gym and getting ready for our first matches. I drank some water and had my banana and so I felt a little renewed energy. I beat my Jimtown opponent by a pin in the second period. He didn't look much bigger than Thirsty and I almost felt a little guilty how easily I handled him.

When we shook hands after the match, he said, "I'm sure glad it was you instead of your sister. I was worried I was going to have to wrestle her and really get clobbered."

I wanted to say that getting pinned in the second period wasn't exactly a great result, either.

I'm glad I didn't because he then said, "I beat you at the beginning of the season in a junior varsity match. You've really gotten better."

I felt bad I hadn't remembered him but was pleased with the compliment. I thought back and realized he was the kid who had long hair earlier in the season and he had edged me, 4-3. He had a buzz-cut now. Maybe he should have read about Samson in the Bible — or at least seen the movie.

In between my first and second matches, I yelled on my teammates, kept myself hydrated and loose and occasionally glanced over into the stands. Wheat, Mom and Lake had joined Dad at some point. I hoped they all saw me win maybe my only match of the day.

Kelly and Sally were there, too, and Kelly was sitting in between Wheat and Sally. When Big Jim had won his first match by a pin, I heard Sally yell out, "That's my big ugly brother who just won!"

My second match was going to be a lot tougher. My opponent was Randy Walker from Riley High School and we had played on the same Little League team. He was pretty good at baseball. I wasn't. He liked giving me wet willies — sticking a slobbery finger in my ear. He also teased me that I threw like a girl. So I loved it when a girl, Wheat that is, pinned him in our dual meet earlier in the season.

When we came together with the ref before the whistle, he said, "Hey, Wet Willie."

I wasn't going to be intimidated.

So I said, "Hey, loser to a girl." Okay, not very original but the ref thought it was bad enough that he warned us both about poor sportsmanship.

I must have hit a nerve because Randy came out like a locomotive. He had me down and was riding me across the mat before I knew what was going on. When the first period ended, I had barely avoided a pin and was down, 5-0. I rallied after that, though, and with about 20 seconds to go in the match, I escaped one of his holds for a point. I won the match, 8-7.

I think Randy must have used up too much energy in the first period. He was down on his knees and didn't seem like he could get up. It would have been a perfect time to get him back with a wet willie of my own. Instead, I gave him a hand up.

"Good match," he mumbled and looked like a third word would have been too much for him.

I patted him on the back and smiled over into the stands.

I was hoping that Sally wouldn't yell, "That's my little ugly winter formal date who just won!" She didn't but I could see her clapping and I think I heard a few "Woof, woof's" come out of her mouth. Wheat stood and did a fist pump and my parents seemed pretty happy, too.

After that, I watched my teammates battle. We got seven of our 13 wrestlers into the semifinals, including a surprising Benny Goodchild at 120. Maybe I should have stayed at that weight.

We went into the school's cafeteria and I had some more of my snacks and rested on top of the fold-out lunch tables.

Wheat came in and was treated like royalty. When a few of the guys saw her, they started chanting, "Wheat, Wheat, Wheat!" again. She looked embarrassed but I could tell that she liked it.

"Great job, Spank," she said. "I'm not sure I could have handled you in that third period."

"I hardly remember anything about it," I told her and meant it.

I had gone into some kind of zone.

"Listen, I know you have more important things to worry about now but we're going home and bringing back your suit so you can change and we can all go to the dance right after the finals," she said. "I hope they'll let you shower here."

Three of us on the team were going to the winter formal and okayed it with Coach Mathews that we could leave when we were done wrestling. He didn't seem all that wild about us maybe leaving while a few of our teammates were still wrestling in the finals but Tony Mason, our 160-pounder, was on the court and that seemed to work in our favor.

It didn't look like I was going to have to worry about making it past the semifinals anyway. My next match was going to be against

Donnie Thompson of Mishawaka who I had barely avoided getting pinned by in our 120 pound match earlier in the week. He's the one who had beaten Wheat, 3-2, in a holiday invitational.

Somebody had heard that he was really struggling to get down to 113 but that he wanted to wrestle Wheat. He had apparently been given a hard time when he had gone up to 120. A few guys from Penn High School had razzed him that he was trying to avoid Wheat. So he went back to 113. But now instead of facing Wheat, he had me. All that cutting weight only to face me. I almost felt sorry for him. Almost.

With Thirsty long gone from the competition, I was the first one up for our team. Thompson came out for the handshake like he was going to do a war dance.

Wheat had told me to watch if he tried an ankle pick on his first move and he did. And I was ready. He missed and I was able to pull off a single leg takedown and scored a quick two points, just like I had in our first meeting four days ago. But before I had any chance to realize what I had done, he quickly reversed me, also just like our first meeting four days ago.

Then it happened. I heard this horrendous noise that sounded like something out of Jurassic Park. And then I heard what sounded like a splat a little too close to my head. A pungent smell hit my nose as Thompson rolled off me.

He had thrown up and apparently wasn't done. He heaved again and the ref scooted him toward his coach. I don't know what he had eaten before our match but it was not a pretty sight out there on the mat.

I almost got sick myself just by the smell before Coach came out and guided me over to the side. Thompson still apparently wasn't through as his coach and a couple of his Mishawaka teammates led him to the locker room with a towel under his chin.

I looked over in the stands and everybody looked like they were either in shock or were grimacing. Mr. Gunderson came out to clean up the mess on the mat. I immediately marked custodian off my mental list of possible professions.

Then I spied Sally, sitting there in her yellow dress. She pretended like she was heaving and then held her nose. How can someone do that and still look dazzling? That girl is something — and probably all wrong for me.

After a few minutes, the Mishawaka coach came back and said that Thompson was still sick and would have to forfeit. He wasn't going to be able to get back on the mat in the three-minute time requirement.

"I didn't know it but his older brother sneaked in a pepperoni and onion pizza after his second match," his coach said to Coach Mathews, the ref and me. "He ate the whole dang thing. I guess he got tired of being hungry. I should have never let him talk me into letting him go back down to 113. I think he just wanted to beat your sister, son. He'll be back at 120 for the rest of the season."

After that news, the ref grabbed my hand and stuck it in the air. I was going to the finals! I jumped into the air. Mr. Gunderson was still on the mat spraying it down and I almost tripped over him. Before I could hustle over to my whooping and hollering teammates, Mr. Gunderson got off his knees and stood in my way.

I thought he was going to congratulate me but he gave me a stare and said, "Did you make this mess?"

"No, but it sure helped me," I said.

He just shook his head and said, "Jeez, you wrestlers are a strange breed."

He was probably right and I was heading through a gauntlet of that kind of breed, all slapping my back and grabbing my shoulders. After I broke away, I headed over to the far end of the gym where my stuff was.

Wheat scampered over and said, "Great first move, Spank. But what happened to Thompson?"

"Ate a whole pizza, according to his coach. He had gotten so hungry trying to cut weight so he could face you. I guess he went a little crazy. I guess you could say that you had a hand in my victory."

"Serves him right," Wheat added and then high-fived me. "Hey, you're going to the finals."

That I was. About that time we looked over at the second mat and watched the Adams wrestler, Terry Dibbits, the guy who acted badly after losing to Wheat in our dual meet, hold on for a victory. He would be my opponent.

"I think you can beat him, Spank," she said. "Oh, and by the way, your date told me to tell you to save some energy for the dance floor. She's a bit of a loon in my opinion but Kelly and her are friends and she is pretty enthusiastic about the wrestling. Too bad Big Jim lost in the second round."

"I'm just hoping to survive the day," I said.

We went back to watch Dion Borden wrestle. After he won, I found a folding chair and sat down. I tried to relax and closed my eyes. When I opened them, Dibbits was staring over at me from where the Adams wrestlers had stationed themselves. He apparently wanted to engage me in a stare-down but I wasn't interested.

CHAPTER 24

I had about a half hour, I figured, before my match. I tried not to look over at Sally in the stands. When the semifinals were over, we had advanced four wrestlers to the finals and still had a slim chance of winning the meet.

I drank some more water, took a dab of honey out of my jar and then headed for the bathroom. I did my stretching and even did a little jogging in the auxiliary gym before Thirsty fetched me for the team meeting. Coach said if all four of us in the finals — me, Borden, Winkler and Mason — won our matches that we could win the meet.

Then he let Wheat say a few words. With a lot of emotion wrapped up in her, she couldn't get out many words. Her battle cry at the end was "Kick the snot out of them!" and that worked for me.

Before the championship round, all of the wrestlers formed two lines and walked across the mat when their names were called and shook the hands of their opponents. I said, "Good luck" to Dibbits as we did our quick handshake and he mumbled something in return.

The 106-pounders then started off the action. I jumped up and down on the side of the mat getting ready to go. The little Mishawaka guy with the long name, who had quickly pinned Thirsty earlier in the week, ended up beating his opponent from Penn, 6-2.

So now it was my turn. I definitely had Hummingbird Heart. Both Dibbits and I went out, listened to same stuff the ref always says and shook hands again.

"Wish it was your sister," he said.

"So do I," I answered.

And then the ref blew the whistle. I did hear Sally yell, "Go get 'em Sir William!" before Dibbits quickly went for a takedown by going for my legs. But I held him off, worked around him and I got a takedown on a fireman's carry. But he quickly broke free for an escape. It was 2-1 my favor.

Dibbits went for me again and this time instead of trying to take me down, he got under me and had me off the ground. We then both went crashing down and my face slammed into the mat with my head gear even flying off. I felt like I had been hit by a bolt of electricity right to the mouth.

And while I tried to keep Dibbits from maneuvering me onto my back, I heard the ref yell, "Time-out. He lost his headgear and one of his front teeth."

"Who?" I yelled.

"You!" he said.

That explained the pain. Coach came out with a towel to stop the blood and started yelling that I had been "slammed." If I couldn't continue and the ref saw it that way, too, then I would win by forfeit. But I wanted to continue.

While a doctor, who was working the meet, came out and looked at my tooth, both coaches were in a heated discussion with the ref, who eventually went over to the scorer's table to talk to the official running the clock.

Coach came over to me to see how I was doing. "You okay?" he asked.

I wanted to say, "Yeah, I just lost one of my front teeth and the guy on the other side of the mat wants to knock my other one out but I'm okay."

Instead, I said, "Sure, Coach, I'm okay."

But the doctor said, "No, you're not, son. You're not wrestling anymore tonight. Too much blood and your whole tooth came out — roots and all."

I hung my head. But Coach said, "Hang in there, Spank, you might win anyway. It looked like an illegal slam to me."

But the two officials thought otherwise. When the one working the mat came over to see how I was, the doctor told him I couldn't continue.

"Tough break, son," he said and then went over and held Dibbit's hand in the air.

My team and supporters didn't take it very well. There was some booing but I just shrugged and shook Dibbits' hand. I'm not sure he would have done the same if our roles were reversed.

My parents and Wheat met me as the doctor ushered me off.

"You need to take him in and have his tooth refitted tonight. See if you can get in contact with your dentist or you'll have to go into the ER. Let me find where the tooth went."

It was another family group hug with Sally lingering off to the side.

"I'd give you a big kiss, handsome, but I don't want to get blood on the dress you like so much," she said.

I pulled away from my parents and said, "I'm heading to the dentist. I'm probably not going to be able to take you to the dance now."

"I understand," she said.

Then Wheat butted in while guiding Kelly Carson over.

"I've got an alternate plan. I'll go with my brother to the hospital and Kelly and Sally can go to the formal. It seems a shame that Sally got all dressed up with nowhere to go."

I figured Sally or Kelly would object a little but they stayed silent.

So I said, "Wheat, you need to go. Maybe the three of you could go."

"Nope, three's a crowd. Sally and Kelly are buds anyway. They'll have fun."

"Sounds okay to me if Kelly is okay with it," Sally said a little more nonchalantly than I would have preferred.

"You sure that's what you want, Tanda?" Kelly asked.

"Yep, we'll do it another time," she said and gave him a pat on the butt.

I guess girls can do that to boys but boys — at least good boys — wouldn't think about doing that to girls. A subject for another time.

Sally came over to me, leaned gingerly over so as not to get any blood on her dress and gave me a peck on the cheek.

"You did good, Sir William," she said. "Get that tooth back in and I'll see you on the dance floor Monday night."

And with that, she grabbed Kelly by the arm and they headed out of the gym.

"I'm so sorry I ruined your night," I said to Wheat.

"I don't think I'm really into dances even if we do know how to dance," she said. "And we'll have to wait and see how much I'm into Kelly. It might just be a passing infatuation on both our parts. We'll see. How you feeling, by the way?"

"A little disappointed, but a little relieved, too," I said. "Although I wish I could have ended my day without losing my tooth. It hurts like heck."

"You were great today, by the way," she said.

Our parents, who had stepped back while we had our little teenage powwow, joined us again and Lake, in Mom's arms, pointed to me and said, "Ouchie."

"Only when I smile," I said and smiled anyway.

We started to leave when Maddie Hamilton came rushing up to us.

"Spank, you may want this," she said and handed me my tooth. "The doctor gave it to me for safe keeping. I cleaned it up a little. You did great."

She smelled great and I suddenly realized that she was wearing some Midnight Breeze as she started off.

I wanted to say something to her but Dibbits came rushing up to us. First, he grabbed Wheat and gave her a big hug. Then he looked at me and my bloody mouth and let out what could only be called a sob — a theatrical one, I'm sure. He embraced me, too, and put his head on my shoulder. I patted him on the back and looked over at a really perplexed Wheat.

Lake decided he wanted in on this hug, too, and Mom gave him to Dibbits, who kissed Lake on the top of the head. Then he went over and hugged Mom and started to do the same to Dad, who stuck out his hand for a shake before that could happen.

After a final fist bump with me, he trotted back to his team area and did a flip before beating on his chest and jumping in the middle of a scrum of teammates. Although I guess we knew how he felt, he never said one word that whole time.

"What is he, a mime?" Dad asked sarcastically.

"I don't know," Wheat said. "But I bet he isn't so friendly when I kick his butt next time we meet."

———

That night after our dentist successfully reinserted my tooth, Wheat was talking quietly on the cell phone while I were getting ready for bed — my mouth still throbbing.

When she hung up, I said, "Kelly?"

"Yep. He asked me out for next week but I said I would have to wait and see how I feel."

"Playing hard to get, aren't you?"

"Naaa. Like I said earlier, I'm just not totally sure how I feel about him. He's not a bad guy, and really nice to look at, but I'm starting to think that he's more impressed with the fact that I can take him down than anything else about me. We'll see. I might give him a chance."

"Big of you," I said.

"Kelly also said that Sally kept talking about how good of a dancer you are even though he said he isn't all that bad. himself. I think he was getting a little tired hearing about Sir William."

"Do you think losing my tooth is a good enough excuse to miss dance lessons Monday? I think she may be too much for me. I can't really be her type, can I? I would be lying if I said he she doesn't give me goosebumps at times but, honestly, she scares the heck out of me, too."

"Well, I hate to add to your woman problems but Laurie Middlebrook sent you a text a few minutes ago while I was talking to Kelly. I didn't mean to read it but I don't think you've ever gotten a text before and I assumed it was for me."

I grabbed the phone away from her and read Laurie's message:

"Spank, I'm so, so sorry how things turned out. It was a mistake going with David to the dance. He's changed so much. Maybe I could treat you at Mug and Munchies sometime if you will forgive me for bowing to my dad's request. For whatever reason, I was voted the winter formal queen — which I guess is a big deal for a sophomore — but it wasn't as fun as it would have been with you. Look forward to seeing you in English class. Laurie."

Wheat was looking over my shoulder at the whole message.

"I've never seen such a long text from a kid before," she said. "She must really like you."

I didn't care at that point. I got into bed. She climbed into the top bunk.

Finally, she said, "Who are you going to dream about tonight, Sir William?"

I waited for a few seconds and then said, "Maybe Maddie Hamilton and I'm getting my own cell phone." Then I quickly wrapped my pillow around my ears so I couldn't hear her.

All I could hear was my Hummingbird Heart anyway.

EPILOGUE

I like to look out my room's second-floor window at the big pond in our back yard. Notre and Dame are out there. At least I hope they still are. It seems a great place for them and they deserve it. They did get me an A for my biology project — Dame out-jumped Notre after being kept in warmer water.

Our new house seems a great place for us, too. Yeah, Wheat and I have our own rooms. I kept my same decor plus a little wrestling trophy for winning the sectional at 113 pounds after missing a couple of meets because of my tooth. I got smeared in the regional the next week, though. But I got the team's Most Improved Award, just like my Little League days.

Wheat couldn't wrestle the rest of the season after her run-in with the One-Booted Man. She did need the plastic surgery for her cheek area. She looks as good as new. And she's back to training — making me run with her, of course.

The end of the school year is only two weeks away and we've been in our new house for almost a month. Mom has a great big kitchen on the first floor and Dad actually has a man cave that he says is mine, too. I would say it has a sports bar-locker room theme. Mom says she likes it best when its door is shut.

Besides the pond, we have a barn because our new home is a converted farmhouse. The barn actually has a basketball goal in it. That's not a big deal to me but maybe Lake will use it and become an NBA star.

I know Wheat likes having the privacy of her own room even though we still share a bathroom and Lake uses it, too. He's out of diapers now, which is a pretty big deal. He can even sit on the toilet but he needs one of us to wipe him when he's done. Slow but sure progress.

He can also climb up into the top bunk in my room (I got the bunks, Wheat got a new queen bed). Sometimes, he wants to sleep with me but Mom is afraid he will fall out of the top bunk. I love my little brother but I'm not going to move up there just so he can sleep below me. He still talks to himself during a lot of the early morning hours.

I do miss talking to Wheat just before we turned off the lights but it's for the best that we no longer share a room. We're getting too old for that. I just hope we stay as close as we are now. I don't know if I told you that I resented her at first because she seemed to be able to do about everything I couldn't when we were 11 … and 12 … and 13 … You get the idea.

But now, I feel like we are almost like twins with a little bit of that ESP going on between us. We both protested when we found out we were moving — me probably a little more since Wheat still had the funeral home woolies. We've both adjusted.

We're only 12 minutes away from our old house but it seems like we're in another world at times because of us being out in the country — or at least on the edge of town. We even have to ride the school bus to Clay. No riding with Big Jim anymore.

Wheat has been seeing Kelly but it's not like they're going steady. And when he shows up in his yellow Mustang, Dad always makes sure that he looks Kelly in the eye and says, "I'm counting on you to drive safely." I think that does the trick.

I was going to ask out Maddie Hamilton but Dion beat me to it. I see them walking down the hall together, sometimes holding hands outside. I'm happy for them.

Sally is still Sally. I got my own cell phone and we talk a lot in the evenings. Maybe I should say she talks and I listen. I think she looks at me as her own junior psychiatrist. I'm not sure anyone has really listened to her before. Yeah, she still calls me Sir William. I think I'm more a buddy to her than some kind of boyfriend. I know she likes me, though, and I do sort of like her, too. She flunked her driver's test a second time so I'm sort of safe from going on any kind of date with her.

That brings us to Laurie. She and I did set up another Coke date before we moved. But she stood me up. She said it was a family emergency — maybe her dad getting his ear slammed in her door while eavesdropping on her calls to me.

Jenny the Waitress — real name Jenny Jenkins — sat down with me after I was alone in one of The Mug's booths for about a half hour. She gave me a ride home when her shift was over. Then she asked me to a movie for later. I think she was feeling sorry for me.

Jenny is set to graduate from Clay but she is only 16 months older than me. When she lived down the street from us, she actually babysat Wheat and me a couple of times when we were 11. I think Mom just wanted to make sure we had a referee or that maybe Wheat would beat me up if we were left alone.

I'm not going to tell you her weight class or where she falls on my 10-point scale. I'm trying to break myself of those habits. Okay, okay, she would be in Thirsty's weight class and could probably handle him.

She and I go to a movie or the mall about once a week now. I think we like each other's company. She picks me up in her old car she bought herself. It's not much better than the clunker that the One-Booted Man drove but that's okay. We've started doing goodnight kisses, which gives me Hummingbird Heart of course. Maybe not on quite the level as Sally's but I'm not complaining.

Wheat seems happy for me, but we don't say much about Jenny. Nor do I bring up Ken … I mean Kelly — ha, ha — much either.

On the drive home, Jenny and I go by a cemetery. She mentioned the other evening that her grandmother had been buried there a few months earlier. I told her my father was there, too. Without saying anything, she made a quick turn into its entrance.

"You go say hello to your daddy," she said.

Mom and I always go to his grave on his birthday in October but that's about it. This was the first time I was there alone. Jenny was about 50 yards away at her grandma's memorial.

I did what she told me to do.

"Hi Dad," I said. "I just wanted you to know that Mom and I are doing great and that we live closer to you now. Thanks so much for putting me on the right track in life and for loving me and Mom. I know you would love Wheat and Ric and Lake, too. I figure you are looking over all of us. Life is really great right now and I'm really not much of a wimp anymore. I'll come more often. See you. Love, Billy Ray."

On the way home, I laid my head on Jenny's shoulder and sobbed a little. We kissed after she pulled into our driveway. When we smooch like that, I don't want to be turned into a Prince Charming anymore. I like being just who I am right now — which includes being up to 118 pounds.

I was probably still a little teary-eyed when I went into the house.

Wheat looked at me and said, "You doing okay?"

"Positively perfect," I said, not wanting to end this story without using alliteration one more time.

ABOUT THE AUTHOR

Bill Moor, a Kokomo native and I.U. grad, wrote for the South Bend Tribune for 48 years. He and his wife Margaret have three children and eight grandchildren.